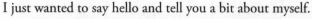

Hi there,

I just wanted to say hello and tell you a bit about myself.

I live on the very outside of London near the River Thames, with my husband (who is Dutch and makes great pancakes!) and our two young daughters. We also have a Siamese cat called Hamish who came to us as a very timid rescue cat and spent the first few weeks hiding up the chimney! Now he is a real family cat and loves sitting on my lap (and trying to sit on my keyboard!) when I'm at my desk writing.

I'm half Welsh and half English but I grew up in Scotland. Before I became a writer I worked as a doctor, mainly with children and teenagers. From as far back as I can remember I've always loved stories in any form – reading books, watching films, playing make-believe games. As a child I always had one fantasy world or another on the go and as I grew older that changed to actual ongoing sagas that I wrote down in exercise books and worked on for weeks at a time.

I really hope you enjoy reading this – ar~~.300 122 224~~
to me at **Gwyneth.Rees@bloomsbury.com**
you think. I'd love it if you told me a bit ab~~.~~

Best wishes,

Gwyneth

Books by Gwyneth Rees

Cherry Blossom Dreams
The Honeymoon Sisters
Earth to Daniel

For younger readers:
The *Fairy Dust* series
Cosmo and the Magic Sneeze
The Magic Princess Dress
My Super Sister
My Super Sister and the Birthday Party

THE MUM HUNT

Gwyneth Rees x

BLOOMSBURY
LONDON OXFORD NEW YORK NEW DELHI SYDNEY

Bloomsbury Publishing, London, Oxford, New York, New Delhi and Sydney

This edition published in Great Britain in February 2017 by
Bloomsbury Publishing Plc
50 Bedford Square, London WC1B 3DP

First published in 2003 by Macmillan Children's Books
a division of Macmillan Publishers Ltd

www.bloomsbury.com

BLOOMSBURY is a registered trademark of Bloomsbury Publishing Plc

A CIP catalogue record for this book is available from the British Library

ISBN 978 1 4088 8263 4

Typeset by RefineCatch Limited, Bungay, Suffolk
Printed and bound in Great Britain by CPI Group (UK) Ltd, Croydon CR0 4YY

1 3 5 7 9 10 8 6 4 2

For Agnès, with love

Chapter One

It all started in French. Well, sort of. I was sitting in French, which was our last lesson that day, feeling fidgety because I'd already finished my work and I had nothing left to do. I was dying to speak to Holly. Holly is my best friend and I'd been waiting all day to ask her advice about something. Holly is an expert at knowing what to do in difficult situations. She says it's because her mum treats her like a grown-up and lets her watch anything she wants on TV and ask any questions she wants about it afterwards. Sometimes Holly and her mum stay up late discussing all sorts of things, which makes me really envious because I'm not allowed to stay up late to discuss anything at all.

Anyway, Holly had been away at the dentist all morning, otherwise I'd have spoken to her earlier. If we'd had an afternoon break I'd have spoken to her then, but our school has abolished afternoon breaks so we can finish earlier like they do on the Continent or something. That means we're expected to go from lunchtime until three o'clock without talking to each other, which if you ask me is a form of *child abuse*. Well, it is for me. I'm a bit of a chatterbox, at least, that's what Dad says. Matthew, my brother, calls me a stuck record which I object to because it implies that I say the same things over and over again, which I don't. He says our great-aunt Esmerelda could talk the hind leg off a donkey too, and that's why I got named after her, but Dad says I got named after her because my mother really liked the name. Nobody calls me Esmerelda, though. They all call me Esmie for short.

Anyway, that afternoon we'd been set an exercise by our French teacher, Miss Murphy (who'd left the room to sort out the teacherless class next door) that involved translating a whole list of different types of food from English into French.

'Guess what?' I hissed, leaning over to see how my friend was getting on with her answers.

'Get off!' Holly pushed my hand away as I tried to pencil in the word *pomme* for her next to apple. 'I *can* do this myself, you know, Esmie!'

'Sorry.' It's just that Juliette, our au pair, is French, and I've started getting top marks in French at school ever since she came. Holly swears she's not jealous but she gets pretty annoyed with me for always finishing things before she does.

'Last night Juliette came up with this idea – and I want to know what *you* think of it!' I announced.

Holly looked at me. I knew that would get her attention.

But I wanted to tell her the whole story – from the beginning – so I did.

'It started when Juliette said something in French that Matthew didn't understand but I did.' I began, proudly. (Dad has this idea that he can use Juliette to turn Matthew and me into fluent French speakers overnight if he gets her to talk to us in nothing but French. Unfortunately Juliette came to England to practise her English, so there's been a bit of a clash.)

Holly crinkled up her nose. 'I think it's really daft, your dad making you talk French every meal time.'

'It's not *every* meal time. We're allowed to speak English at breakfast and lunch and all day if we want at the weekends. Anyway, Matthew didn't understand her and I did!'

'So?' Holly grunted, going back to her work. Holly doesn't understand what it's like to have to compete all

3

the time with an older brother for your parent's attention. She's eleven like me, but she's an only child. Her parents are divorced and they compete with each other all the time for *her* attention. They had a big fight about who would get custody of her and now it's shared, so Holly spends one night a week and every second weekend with her dad and the rest of the time with her mum. She's got two of everything: two bedrooms, two wardrobes and two toothbrushes. The only thing she hasn't got two of yet is mothers and fathers. Neither of her parents has found anyone else, though Holly reckons it won't be long before one of them does and she's dreading that.

I continued to talk despite the fact that she looked like she wasn't listening. 'We were sitting eating our dinner when Juliette started telling Dad – in French – all about an advert she'd seen in the lonely-hearts column of that free newspaper that comes through the door. Juliette said he should answer it. Dad nearly choked on his *pommes de terre.*' I pointed to the empty space on Holly's page next to potatoes and waited for her to fill it in.

'What did your dad say?' Holly put down her pencil, looking interested now.

'Something in French I didn't understand but I think it was pretty rude. Then the telephone rang and it was

4

Dad's work and they'd just found a dead body or something and that ruined everything as usual. But then, after he'd gone out, Juliette showed us the advert and –'

'A *dead body*?' Holly always gets excited by any gruesome details I let out about Dad's work. Dad is a police detective which Holly reckons is really cool. 'Was it murdered?'

'How should I know?' I wasn't meant to know about it at all and Dad would kill me if he knew I was talking about it to Holly. 'Look, never mind that! I want to know what you think about *this*.' I rummaged around in my schoolbag and pulled out a crumpled piece of newspaper, but before I could show it to her our French teacher strode back into the room and stopped at the first desk she came to.

Which happened to be ours …

'What's this?' Before I knew what was happening she had grabbed the lonely-hearts column from my hand.

I was horrified. Miss Murphy is fortyish, with round spectacles and very flat hair and she looks like she wouldn't know what to do with a lonely heart if it jumped out and hit her in the face. And she couldn't possibly miss *this* lonely heart because it was ringed with Juliette's red pen.

'It's her dad's, Miss,' Holly said, quickly, pointing at me.

I scowled at her. The rest of the class had stopped talking and the silence was horrible. I could feel them all staring.

'Is that right, now?' Miss Murphy has a really strong Irish accent and she wears a big silver cross round her neck which Holly says means she's a Catholic. I don't know much about religion seeing as how Dad never takes us to church. Holly doesn't go to church either, but, like I said before, her mum talks to her a lot about things.

Miss Murphy began to read the advertisement out loud, slowly, like she was just a beginner reader. '"Beautiful, blue-eyed, blonde botanist WLTM ..."' she recited, raising her voice so she could still be heard above the sniggers coming from everybody else. 'W ... L ... T ... M ...' she repeated, carefully. She looked at both of us for help.

Holly nudged me. 'Esmie.' Like I was the expert.

'Would Like To Meet,' I croaked, feeling so embarrassed I wanted to die.

'Would like to meet "a handsome, plant-loving, man in uniform"!' Miss Murphy let out a noise like a muffled snort, which is a habit of hers. Our class were all laughing really loudly now. 'Do you think these criteria would be fitting your daddy, then, Esmie?'

I was bright red and trembling by this time. I could have killed Holly. Why couldn't she just have said we'd *found* the paper or something?

I shook my head, helplessly. I was so embarrassed I couldn't even speak.

'He's no good with plants, Miss,' Holly said.

The whole class laughed even louder.

'But he *is* a policeman!' Holly added, starting to sound like she was enjoying herself.

'Is that so?' Miss Murphy's eyes were sparkling wickedly. 'Well, it sounds like this …' She glanced again at the advert. '… this "lady botanist" prefers men in uniform, so maybe he's still in with a chance!'

'Only he's plain clothed, Miss,' Holly put in, frowning. 'Isn't he, Esmie? He's a detective, Miss, so he has to be plain clothed so his murderers don't recognise him.'

I found my voice then. 'That's not true!' I spluttered. 'He has to show his murderers his badge before he asks them anything!' Goodness knows why I said that.

Miss Murphy's face went pink and she started to chortle. It wasn't a pretty sight. 'Well, perhaps if he's got a badge, that will make up for him not having a uniform,' she teased.

'Only if it's a really *sexy* badge!' one of the boys called out.

I wanted to crawl under my desk and never come out again. Or at the very least, move out of the area and change my name so no one would ever be able to trace me.

As the bell rang, Miss Murphy shouted at the class that for our homework she wanted us to write out pretend advertisements to go in a French lonely-hearts column. Then she started laughing again. She gave the advertisement back to me and rushed out of the classroom, no doubt in order to tell everyone in the staffroom.

'Holly, *why* did you have to do that?' I snapped, as I stuffed the piece of newspaper as far down into the bottom of my bag as it would go.

'Don't blame me!' she said, looking offended. 'He's *your* father!'

'Hey, Esmie?' one of the boys called out to me.

I looked up. It was Billy Sanderson, who usually only speaks to me when he wants to copy my homework and then acts all spiteful for the rest of the week because I won't let him. He was standing in the doorway with all his mates.

'Miss Murphy's single! What do you reckon? Shall we introduce her to your dad? Then you could have her for a stepmum!'

8

All his mates laughed. I saw that Holly was smirking again too.

I gritted my teeth. That's when I started to feel sick. My head started to hurt and I felt a bit dizzy.

I picked up my schoolbag and pushed past them, out of the room. I really didn't feel well. And I started to think of all the terrible illnesses I could have that would mean I'd never be able to come back to school ever again.

Chapter Two

'Juliette, I think I might have meningitis,' I said, dumping my schoolbag on the floor and flopping down on to the settee as soon as I got home. 'I've got a terrible headache and I feel really sick. I think maybe I've got a temperature.'

Juliette, who was doing a pile of ironing, put down the iron and came to feel my forehead with the back of her hand. Juliette is twenty-two and really pretty. She's got short blonde hair, cropped just like the models in *Vogue* magazine, and blue eyes with long dark eyelashes. I wish *I* looked more like Juliette. I've got brown eyes and brown hair that's dead straight and comes to my shoulders, and people are always saying that I look really pale.

'You don't feel hot,' Juliette said, removing her hand from my brow.

'That's because I'm cold,' I said, shivering abruptly. 'I'm going to bed. Will you tell Dad I'm not well when he comes in?' I made a big thing of dragging myself off the settee.

'When I've finished this, I will come and see what you want,' Juliette called after me.

I thought the very least she could have done was make sure I didn't faint on the stairs but then Juliette never seems to make a fuss of me that way. No one does. Dad just gets all panicky whenever I'm ill and Matthew just goes, 'Yuck. Germs!', and keeps out of my way. I reckon if my mother was here, she'd make a *huge* fuss of me. My photo of my mother stands right by my bed and when I'm in bed I talk to her and she's always really understanding. I told her about today as I got undressed, and about how sick I felt, and I knew she thought that I should definitely stay off for the rest of the week and get myself truly better.

I got into bed and rested my head against the pillow. I felt thirsty.

'Darling, I think you should be drinking plenty of fluids,' my mother said, smiling at me silently.

I climbed out of bed and headed groggily for the landing. 'JULIETTE!' I yelled. 'I want a drink!'

Juliette poked her head out of the living room and glared at me. 'Juliette, will you *please* bring me a drink,' she corrected me, sternly, like being polite really mattered when you were dying of meningitis.

'Orange squash, *please*,' I croaked, swaying dangerously at the top of the stairs.

Juliette sighed, loudly. 'You had better go back to bed. I will bring it up to you.'

I felt tears prick the backs of my eyes. Juliette didn't care about me. I was just a way of making money as far as she was concerned. I ran back to my bedroom and slammed the door. By the time Juliette reached me I was buried under the covers and pretending to be asleep.

'Esmie, here is your drink.' I heard it clink against my mother's picture as she set it down.

I could hear her standing there trying to work out if I really was asleep. I heard her starting to walk out of the room when I felt overcome by a surge of anger. I sat bolt upright in bed. 'Don't bother checking to see if I'm still *alive* or anything, will you?!' I snarled.

She looked shocked. 'Still alive?'

'Yes. I mean, people can die pretty fast from meningitis!'

'Meningitis?' She looked even more puzzled.

'That's right! I mean, you're not a doctor, are you? You don't know for sure that I *haven't* got meningitis!'

12

'Esmie, why are you behaving like this? You are not so sick to have meningitis. Something has happened to make you like this. What is it?' She came and stood close to my head, so close that she was standing in front of my glass of orange juice and the photo of my mother. 'Tell me,' she said, crouching down by my bed and touching my head. 'What is wrong?'

I stared at her. I felt all funny inside.

I opened my mouth to say something angry and instead I burst into tears.

Juliette was really different from all our other au pairs right from the beginning. From the day she arrived she chatted to Dad in a way that none of the others ever did. For instance, she chatted to him about why she reckoned he never had any success in his relationships. Dad has dated a few women in the past few years but nothing's ever lasted more than a few months. In fact, mostly you're talking weeks, not months. He hadn't gone out with anyone in ages, and then, a few weeks after Juliette arrived, he got set up on a blind date.

The date was arranged by one of Dad's friends. When Dad got home from that evening, it was so early that we were all still up. Dad looked positively traumatised, and

Juliette made him relate the whole encounter over a soothing mug of cocoa. I was really pleased. Normally I never get to hear anything about Dad's dates. It sounded like this one had been going all right until the part where his date had asked about my mother and Dad had replied that she was the most beautiful creature he'd ever met and the one great love of his life (or something really slushy like that).

Juliette had gasped in horror. 'But that is *terrible*! It is no wonder you put her off!'

'Well anything else would be a lie!' Dad replied, stubbornly, flushing a little. 'And lying is no way to start off a relationship!'

'Well, you will never start a relationship unless you lie about *this*! Can you not think of something less ... less *aggressive* ... to say to these poor women if they are unfortunate enough to ask?'

'You don't mean "aggressive", Juliette, you mean "passionate"!' I put in, helpfully, but everyone ignored me.

'You could always tell them she was ... I don't know ... *sweet*!' volunteered Matthew, who was taking advantage of Dad's temporary state of distraction by standing in front of the fridge with the door open, swigging back orange juice straight from the carton.

'Holly's mum says it's an insult to be called "sweet" unless you're lying in a pram wearing a bonnet,' I chipped in again. I turned pointedly to address Juliette. '*She* reckons Dad mucks up all his dates because deep down he's *scared* of falling in love again.'

'Holly's mother should mind her own business,' Dad grunted.

'But there is sense in what she says, no?' Juliette insisted. 'It is scary to fall in love. Especially when you have lost someone.'

Dad visibly swallowed. He never talks about losing my mother. He talks a lot about being *with* her, but never about losing her. Juliette says it's typically English not to want to talk about the feelings that you have deep inside. I'm not sure if it's typically English but I am sure that it's typically *Dad*.

Anyway, Juliette had certainly changed things in our house. She was a lot more interfering than all our other au pairs, and sometimes I worried that Dad wouldn't be able to take it any more and would send her back to France. For one thing, she was always suggesting ways in which Dad could spend more one-to-one time with Matthew in order to promote male bonding.

'Who does she think she is? Mary Poppins?' Dad

grumbled, the last time Juliette interfered in one of his disagreements with my brother.

'I can just imagine you flying across from France underneath your umbrella,' I told her now, as she gave me a hug and asked me what the matter was. But I couldn't tell her about what had happened in French today. She might go and tell Dad. So I just said I didn't feel well.

Juliette sighed. 'Perhaps something very nice will happen soon.' She stroked my hair. 'You never know. Your father is an attractive man. He may very well get married again and then you will have a nice new step-mother. Would you like that?'

'Yes, but Dad won't ever get married again,' I said. 'He still loves my mother too much. He doesn't *want* to replace her with anyone else – at least that's what Holly's mother says.'

'What about Holly's mother?' Juliette asked, suddenly. 'She is single too, is she not?'

'No way!' I shrieked, sitting up in bed and forgetting all about my meningitis. 'There is no way Dad and Holly's mother ... For one thing, Dad hates her!'

'*Hates* her?' Juliette looked even more interested. 'Hate is a very *passionate* emotion, no?'

'You mean "aggressive", Juliette!' I corrected her, but she just smiled, like she knew things that I didn't about life in general.

'I know exactly what I mean,' she said, firmly. 'Now you – with your bad head – should get some rest, I think.' And she winked at me as she left my room.

Chapter Three

'Dad!' I called out, running downstairs as soon as I heard his key in the lock. I'd rested so much after I'd got home from school that I wasn't the least bit sleepy now that it was actually time for bed.

I had been sitting on the top stair waiting for him. It was already half an hour past my bedtime, which Dad is a bit of a stickler about. He says he has to be a stickler about everything because there's only one of him, but I don't know. My brother says he reckons Dad would still be throwing his weight around like an astronaut in a space shuttle, whether we had a second parent or not. I reckon he's probably right. I mean, I'll give you meal times as an example. Dad's really rigid about everything. He doesn't like us leaving any food on our plates, even if it's only enough to provide a very small snack for any starving children who happen to be passing, and he likes us to ask permission before we leave the table. And he won't let me have even the smallest drop of wine to taste, no matter how much I go on about the children in France drinking it and what about European unity? I mean, Holly's mother doesn't make a fuss about any of those things and she's a single parent too, isn't she? Matty says Dad's just plain old-fogeyish when it comes to table manners and I think he's right.

'What are you doing still up?' Dad asked, giving me a hug and looking pleased to see me just the same.

'I don't feel well. Juliette thinks I should stay off school tomorrow.' That wasn't really a lie. I mean, for all I knew, she might think that and just not be saying it because she didn't want to worry me.

'Where *is* Juliette?' he asked, frowning. My brother was playing some music in his room which didn't bother me, but I could tell Dad thought it was too loud.

'Washing her hair,' I told him. Juliette has her own bathroom next to her bedroom and she tends to spend a lot of time in it after she thinks I'm in bed. 'Dad, I've got a question for you. Do you like brunettes best, or redheads, or blondes?'

'I beg your pardon?'

'I'm filling in a questionnaire,' I said. 'In *marie claire*.'

19

Juliette always had a copy of *marie claire* lying about, and in one of them I'd found an article titled 'How To Choose Your Perfect Partner'.

'Esmie ...' He scratched his head. He was tired, I could see that. 'Esmie, *why* would you possibly need to fill in such a questionnaire?' (*His* hair is dark brown, by the way. With a few grey bits at the sides which Juliette says only make him look more distinguished.)

'I want to find out who your ideal partner would be,' I told him. 'I've been making a list of desirable qualities. Do you want to see it?'

'All I want to see right now is you getting into that bed,' Dad said. 'And if your brother doesn't turn down that racket then that's where I'll be sending him in a minute as well. Come on. Upstairs.'

Dad rapped hard on Matthew's door as we passed. My brother must have known it was Dad because he turned his music down straight away. He'd never do that for me and he always puts up a bit of a fight when Juliette tells him to do stuff too. Matthew, just in case you haven't guessed by now, is a real pain. He's fifteen and he thinks he's really cool. And get this! Holly *fancies* him. She says it's adorable the way his fringe flops down over his eyes and she thinks he's got a really cute bum. So you see, Holly's not right about everything.

'Did you have a good day at work, Dad?' I asked, as I snuggled down into my bed. I always ask him how his day went. It's the sort of thing a wife is meant to say, I reckon, and since Dad hasn't got one, I try my best to fill in.

'Tolerable, thank you, m'dear,' Dad replied, in the funny sergeant-major voice he always puts on when I ask him that.

I giggled. Even though I hate Dad treating me like a little kid, sometimes I really like it when he puts me to bed. We don't tend to see so much of him during the week, so it means I get him all to myself for a few extra minutes.

'Night-night, sweetheart,' he said, in his normal voice as he kissed me on the forehead. 'See you in the morning.'

After he'd gone, I reached out and touched the photo of my mother. I don't do that when Dad's watching because I don't want him to think I'm sad about her. If he thinks I'm sad then he might get sad himself. In the photo, my mother has dark brown hair with no grey bits. I closed my eyes tightly and tried really hard to imagine what her voice sounded like. But no matter how much

I hear her talking to me inside my head, I can't hear her real out-loud voice at all.

By the time Juliette woke me up the next morning Dad had already gone to work. That happens a lot when he's got a difficult case to solve. Matthew had left the house early too. Recently, Matty and his best friend, Jake, had been hanging round with some boys who were a bit older than them. One of them worked in McDonald's and could get them free breakfasts, so Matty had started skipping breakfast at home and going to McDonald's before school instead. Dad didn't know about it but Juliette did and she didn't seem to mind. I reckoned Dad would, because he likes to keep an eye on how much junk food Matthew and I are eating, but I wasn't about to tell him since this way I got to have Juliette all to myself at breakfast time.

Juliette asked how I was feeling, and I told her I didn't feel nearly well enough to go to school today, though I reckoned that maybe I didn't have meningitis after all.

Fortunately she was in a sympathetic mood. 'Why don't you stay in bed and I'll bring some breakfast up to you? I have an idea that I want to tell you.'

It turned out that Juliette was still fixated on the idea

of setting Dad up with someone. 'If we cannot persuade your father to *answer* an advert in the lonely hearts then I think we should send one in on his behalf. Perhaps he will feel more confident if these women are the ones writing to *him*,' she said, as she set a tray of juice and cereal in front of me and sat herself down on the end of my bed.

'Don't you think we should tell Dad before we do that?' I asked, feeling worried.

Juliette clicked her tongue, disapprovingly. 'Why? He will never agree. But if it is a *fait accompli* – how do you say that in English?'

'A fate-a-cum-plee,' I said, frowning. 'But what would we put?'

'Tall handsome Englishman ... Wealthy ... Sexy ... Something like that.'

'But that's lying!' I protested. 'Dad isn't wealthy, or ... well ... any of that other stuff!' I felt a bit embarrassed at the very mention of the word 'sexy' in connection with my dad.

Juliette waved her hand dismissively. 'Of course we must put those things! You do not want him to sound boring, do you, and attract all sorts of boring women!' She shuddered.

23

'But Juliette, we have to tell Dad the truth. We have to tell him we're doing it!'

Juliette snorted. 'What is this English obsession with always having to tell the truth? What your father does not know cannot upset him. What he does, can. It is simple! After all, there is plenty of time for him to be upset *after* he finds out what we have done.'

Unfortunately, Juliette's arguments stumped me.

'Anyway,' she added, as she walked out through the door. 'Your father is lonely. Anyone can see that!'

And that got me thinking. I thought about all the evenings when Dad sat downstairs on his own watching television after my brother and I had gone to bed. I remembered all the holidays we'd been on in the past, where Dad had sat on his own on the beach with a book, while my brother and I had raced around enjoying ourselves on the sand.

Dad was always alone. That was just the way it was. I'd never thought of him as being *lonely*.

But what if Juliette was right? What if he *was*?

The next day Juliette took me to the doctor, who said there were a lot of viral infections going around, so I might have caught one of those. I'd started to feel very sick again that morning and I'd nearly thrown up in the waiting room. Our doctor took my temperature, looked at my tongue and peered inside my ears with this metal instrument that I thought she said was called a horror-scope but maybe I didn't hear her right. Anyway, I moaned a bit and said I felt sick while she was examining me, and when she got me up on her couch to feel my tummy I made sure I groaned as soon as she touched it. She looked a bit dubious but wrote me a sick note anyway and said I may as well take the next day or two off school just to be on the safe side. And as soon as I got out of her surgery, I felt much better.

Dad and Matthew had another of their rows that evening. This time it was over whether or not Matthew could get his nose pierced.

'Come on, Dad. Jake's getting his done.' Matthew had him cornered in the kitchen which is never a good idea. Dad tends to get pretty cross if he feels like he can't escape from us easily. 'I won't wear it to school. Just if I'm going out.'

'Yuck!' I said. 'Then you'll have a big hole in your nose at school! That's disgusting!'

'Your Aunt Wendy had a lot of piercings when she was a teenager, but then, she was a punk rocker,' Dad said, lightly, pouring himself some coffee. 'You're not thinking of dyeing your hair pink as well, are you Matthew?'

'Dad, I wish you'd stop pretending you *know* stuff!' My brother glared at Dad like he couldn't believe he hadn't died of old age years ago. 'Jake's dad doesn't interfere in *his* life all the time!'

'*Jake's* dad says it's Jake's nose so he has the right to do what he wants with it,' I added, helpfully. I'd been witness to a rehearsal of how Matthew was going to broach this one with Dad and in my opinion that bit shouldn't be left out.

Dad started to laugh.

Matthew grunted, 'Shut it, Esmie!'

'Did I say your brother's nose didn't belong to him?' Dad joked, reaching across to pinch mine between his fingers and do a pretend nose nab. 'Yours, on the other hand is *all mine*!'

I shrieked as he started tickling me.

Neither of us noticed how cross Matthew was until we heard the front door slam.

Dad sighed. 'I tell you, Esmie. I'm dreading having you turn into a teenager too. Having one in the house is bad enough, but two ...'

'I'll probably be even moodier than Matthew when

I'm a teenager because I'm a girl and my hormones will be more ferocious,' I informed him, solemnly.

He smiled. 'Really? What gave you that idea?'

'Juliette.'

'Juliette. Well, you can tell Juliette from me that she doesn't know what she's talking about. After all, she's never been a boy, has she?'

I shook my head.

'Well, *I* have. Believe me, I know.'

I found myself thinking about Dad as a teenage boy. It was very difficult.

Juliette came into the kitchen, then. She must have overheard us because she was smiling. 'I bet Matthew would like to hear about you as a boy,' she said, lightly.

Dad smiled and said, drily, 'Thanks for the insight, Juliette,' before brushing past us out of the kitchen. It was a pretty ordinary thing for him to say but there was something about the way he said it, and the way he hurried away, that made me feel sort of cut off from him. Dad gets like that sometimes – as if he doesn't want you to know what he's really thinking or feeling.

'Do you still think Dad's lonely?' I asked Juliette. 'I mean, he hasn't *said* he is.'

'Of course he has not said it. He does not want *you* to know that.'

I frowned. Was that it, then? Was it when Dad felt lonely that he hid his feelings from us?

'I don't *want* Dad to be lonely,' I said to Juliette.

Juliette looked at me. 'Well, you know what to do about it, then, don't you?'

Chapter Four

DAMSEL IN DISTRESS SOUGHT BY DISHY DETECTIVE, EARLY FORTIES. MUST LIKE CHILDREN AND ANIMALS.

Juliette looked a bit doubtful as she read out the advert I had come up with after several hours of carefully studying all the ones in the paper. 'But what is "damsel in distress"? And what is "dishy"?' she asked.

'Dad's a sucker for women who need his help,' I explained. 'Especially if they're pretty.' It was true. Dad is always stopping to help if one gets stuck in a stalled car, or if he spots one alone wrestling with a puncture, or if he's walking past one who can't open her car door in the Sainsbury's car park because she's got a baby in one arm and three bags of shopping in the other. I reckon if he met one whose life was in danger and they needed resuscitating, it would make his day! '"Dishy" means

29

"handsome", only it's better than putting "handsome" because it begins with "d" and all the best adverts have all the words starting with the same letter.'

'Do they?' She looked like somebody who suddenly realises they're not such an expert at something as they thought they were. 'But this other part … this "in distress" … We do not want to attract women who might be too … too …' She couldn't think of the English word for whatever it was she was trying to say and in the end she gave up. 'And what is this about animals? There are no animals here!'

'No, but I'd really like a dog!'

'But I am not sure your father would want a dog … or a lady "in distress".'

'It's not a *lady*, Juliette, it's a *damsel*! Trust me on this one, OK?'

Juliette still looked dubious.

'Maybe we shouldn't do this at all,' I said. 'Dad will be pretty mad.'

Juliette seemed to rally. 'Of course we must do it. Your father may be angry but it will not last long. Not when he falls in love and is happy again. Your father is far too cautious in these matters. He needs our help to take a *reesk*.'

'A risk?'

'Yes! A *reesk*.' She looked pleased at the thought. 'After all ...' She grinned. 'What is *lurve* without *reesk*?'

'A whole lot less hassle?' I answered, smartly.

Juliette clicked her tongue, shaking her head in disgust. 'Such Englishness.' She snatched the piece of paper from me. 'I will send this to the newspaper tomorrow. Now ... do you think you are well enough to go back to school this afternoon?'

I gulped. We had double French at school that afternoon. Suddenly I felt dizzy again. I had a tight feeling in my chest. 'Juliette, I need to lie down,' I gasped, clutching the part of my chest where I reckoned my heart should be. I could feel it thumping. Was it normal to be able to feel your own heart thumping or did that mean you were about to have a heart attack?

'I will leave you to recover,' Juliette said – pretty coolly, I thought, considering that she was meant to be in charge of me, which presumably meant she wasn't supposed to let me die if it could possibly be avoided.

I told myself I didn't care. As Juliette turned to leave my room, I closed my eyes and concentrated hard on hearing my mother's voice instead. I could almost feel her looking down on me from heaven. '*I won't ever leave*

31

you, darling,' she said, and her voice was perfect. It was all throaty and beautiful and it reminded me of … I don't know … the voice of Bambi's mother or something.

'Esmie!'

I opened my eyes. Juliette was staring at me from the doorway.

'What is wrong with you?' she said, crossly. 'You act like you are in a trance!'

I giggled. I liked the thought of me in a trance. I closed my eyes again, stuck my arms out horizontally in front of me like a sleepwalker and droned, Dalek-like, 'I-am-in-a-trance. I-do-not-want-to-talk-to-you. Do-not-disturb-me.'

Juliette made an exasperated noise and left me to it.

Juliette got more and more enthusiastic about the advert. She said we should read through all the replies we got and make a shortlist, before showing them to Dad. Then she said it was a pity we couldn't conduct interviews before we let any of these women actually meet Dad so we could eliminate any weirdos at the outset.

I reckoned we should let Dad decide for himself who was a weirdo and who wasn't, but Juliette insisted that once a person started falling in love, there was often no way of stopping them, and that she wouldn't like to rule out the possibility of Dad falling in love with a *beautiful* weirdo. The whole thing was starting to make my head spin. The more Juliette discussed the pros and cons of screening processes that would eliminate axe-wielding psychopaths and interviews that would sift out any women who were just after Dad's money, the more nervous I started to get. Because Juliette was talking like she had no confidence whatsoever in Dad's own taste in women and that if we didn't watch out, I could end up with just about *anyone* for a stepmother.

And then there was the question that I didn't dare ask Juliette, the one that kept popping into my mind before I went to sleep each night. What about my *real* mother? What was she thinking about all this? I mean, there she was, waiting patiently up in heaven for Dad to die one day and go and join her. It wasn't going to be very good, was it, if he got to heaven and had to choose between spending eternity with my mother or with wife number two? Unless wife number two went to hell instead, which would certainly solve the problem, but she couldn't go to hell unless she was bad and, if she was bad, I wouldn't want her as a stepmother, would I?

On Thursday night I was lying in bed, staring at my mother's photograph, worrying about all of this, when something really weird happened. I had just asked my mother if she minded Dad falling in love with somebody else, and as usual she was looking back at me silently with that smile on her face which didn't tell me anything, when the phone started ringing. It was just as if it was *her* ringing me to answer my question. Well, I knew that was a crazy idea and I dismissed it straight away, but then my dad called up the stairs to ask me to come down to the phone, and that got me thinking crazily all over again.

'Who is it?' I called out, as I tramped down the stairs to join him.

'It's a surprise,' he said, smiling.

I took the telephone from him and said, 'Hello?'

'Esmie?' a crackly voice said on the end of the line.

'Grandma!' My grandmother lives in America and we don't get to see her that often. She got divorced from my grandfather years ago, before I was even born, and then, about five years ago, she met this American university professor and got married to him and went out to live with him in Chicago.

'How are you, my angel?' she asked. She was getting an American accent but I knew better than to tell her that.

'I'm fine, Grandma!' I replied. I started to ask her lots

of questions about her three cats and her voluntary work with homeless people.

Dad whispered to me that he was going upstairs to get Matty – my brother never hears the phone when he has his headphones on – and I knew that this was my chance. You see, my grandmother is the one who talks to me most about my mother – she was *her* mother – and it seemed like more than just a coincidence that she was phoning just at the moment when I most wanted my mother's advice.

'Grandma,' I said, quickly, when Dad was out of earshot. 'I'm a bit worried about something. It's to do with Dad.'

There was a short silence on the other end of the line. Then my grandmother asked, 'Has he met someone?', just as if she was telepathic.

'Not yet, but ...' I wished I could explain about the advert and everything but there just wasn't time. '... I think he might be about to.'

'Well,' Grandma sighed, 'if he *does* find the right person – someone who will make him happy and love you and Matthew as well – then I shall be very happy about it.' She paused. 'And I know your mother would be too.'

'*Would* she?' I asked.

'Of course! When you love someone, you want them to be happy, don't you?' Grandma sounded one hundred per cent certain about that.

'I guess so …' I murmured, and then I had to change the subject because Dad and Matthew were coming down the stairs towards me.

As I gave up the phone so that Matthew could have a chance to speak to her, I found that I was feeling a lot calmer inside. And when I went back to bed and looked again at my mother's photograph, I thought she looked more peaceful too. I know it sounds weird but it was almost as if, now that she had found a way of saying what she wanted to say to me, *she* felt much calmer too.

It wasn't until Juliette crept into my room all apologetic looking on Friday night that I realised something had gone seriously wrong with our Lonely Hearts Plan. She was holding the newspaper in her hand.

I sat up quickly. 'What is it? Has Dad found out?'

She shook her head. 'But we did not read the instructions correctly. You do not send your advertisement to the newspaper. You phone. Then they give you another number, which the lonely hearts ring if they want to leave you a message. Look!' She pointed to the bit at the top that we hadn't read properly before – the bit that gave you the complete instructions.

'It's all computerised!' I said, in horror, after I'd pored over the relevant section for several minutes. You had to record a message into a voicemail thing when you sent in your ad. And then if someone liked your advert they rang the number and listened in to your message and if they liked *that* then they could leave you a message back with *their* phone number on it. 'People don't send you letters at all!' I exclaimed.

Juliette sighed. 'The person seeking the partner must record the message for themselves, I think.' She added, hopefully, 'Perhaps if we tell your father he will agree to do it?'

'No way! Dad hates computers! And answering machines! Anyway, he'll be too embarrassed!'

'These English men are easily embarrassed, it is true.'

Just then there was a knock on my door and Dad stuck his head round. He stuck it back again pretty quickly when he saw Juliette. She was dressed in her nightshirt and when I say shirt, I mean shirt. She was wearing a pair of knickers as well, but I guess you probably couldn't tell that from where Dad was standing.

'Esmie, get to sleep,' Dad growled. 'You know you've got a busy day tomorrow. *If* you're feeling up to it, that is.' Dad reckoned it was a bit of a coincidence that I'd suddenly started feeling better on a Friday night just in time for the weekend. 'And Juliette, I'm going into the bathroom now. I'd be grateful if you could streak back across the hall *before* I come out again.'

Juliette raised her eyebrows at me. 'See what I mean? Easily embarrassed, no?'

I giggled and pushed her off my bed, kicking the newspaper off with her. 'Are you coming tomorrow?' I asked her. It was Holly's birthday party tomorrow afternoon and Dad and Juliette had been invited too. Holly always has massive birthday parties with lots of grown-ups there as well as kids. This year they were having a barbecue in their back garden and I was going round early to help get things ready. 'Go on, Juliette! It'll be fun!' I urged her.

'And so will shopping be fun, I think,' Juliette replied, smiling. 'It is my day off, remember? No Esmie for the whole day tomorrow! Aahh!' And she gave a sigh of pleasure like she was sinking into a longed-for hot bath.

I stuck out my tongue at her, and she laughed and blew me a kiss as she slipped out of the door.

Juliette was all right, really. I snuggled down into bed and for once I didn't feel like talking to my mother. But I didn't go to sleep straight away. My mind kept drifting back to something that had happened just now. It was the way Dad had blushed and darted back outside when he saw Juliette, as if he was really embarrassed to see her in her skimpy nightshirt. Holly has this test she does on you if she wants to find out if you fancy someone. She looks straight at you and says the name of the boy she reckons you fancy and if you blush, she takes that as proof that you *do* fancy him. But Dad couldn't fancy Juliette. I mean, she was loads younger than him and she drove him up the wall half the time. Of course, it was true that in movies people were always starting out hating each other and ending up falling in love. But that was in movies. Besides, Dad didn't *hate* Juliette. He'd never said that. I tried to imagine Dad and Juliette doing something romantic like kissing each other. The thought of it made me want to laugh. I had to try really hard to think of something less funny or I knew I'd never get to sleep.

Chapter Five

I woke up next morning and looked at my alarm clock. With any luck Dad would already have left for work. Dad always works whether it's the weekend or not when there's a murder investigation on the go. He doesn't know what a weekend is, if you ask me. Except when we're on holiday. Dad really relaxes when we go away anywhere. He's not a bit like those detectives you get in stories who always manage to get caught up in a murder mystery no matter where they go. Someone could stab *and* strangle *and* shoot someone to death right in front of Dad when we're on holiday and I reckon he still wouldn't stop licking his ice cream. Dad doesn't even like to admit to being a detective if people ask and he usually pretends to be something else like a pharmacist or a financial adviser. Don't ask me why he chooses those two. He says he reckons they sound like really plausible things to be.

I went straight downstairs to the kitchen. The free paper had been delivered and it looked like nobody had opened it yet. I hunted through it until I found the lonely-hearts page and then I took it with me into the living room and picked up the phone.

I was nearly at the end of listening to my tenth advert when Matty came into the room. I didn't hear him at first. '… So, if you'd like to leave me a message, well … well, then please leave me a message …' It was painful, listening to some of them, but I thought it might help to hear the sorts of messages other people leave.

'Esmie! What are you doing?' Matty was staring at me.

I jumped. 'Nothing!' I had already punched in another number and I reckoned it was best not to act too secretive, but before I could start pretending just to be on the phone to a friend he had snatched the receiver from me. 'HEY! GIVE THAT BACK!'

He let out a loud whoop as he realised what I was listening to.

'*Matthew!* What are you doing?' Juliette came charging into the room and snatched the telephone. After listening herself for a couple of seconds she slammed it down and glared at both of us. 'What are you thinking of? These phone calls are not free! And your father – on his

41

bill he has all the calls written out, each one separately …
Each one … Each one …'

'Itemised?' I supplied, sheepishly.

'Exactly!' She spun round to glower at me. 'And now
he will ask who has been phoning this expensive number
behind his back!' She grabbed the paper to verify just
how expensive it was and her face went pink. 'See how
much it is every minute? Look!' And she threw it back at
me, looking like she was thoroughly disgusted.

'It's OK. He'll just think it was Matty,' I attempted
to reassure her. 'Matty's always phoning up those dodgy
chatline numbers whenever his friends come round.'

'I am not!' My brother stopped grinning.

'Yes, you are! Dad said if you didn't stop lying
about it he was going to start checking the phone for
fingerprints!'

'Esmie, stop it!' Juliette gasped. 'I do not wish for
more arguments between Matthew and your father! It is
much too boring!'

'You don't mean "boring", Juliette, you mean –' I
began, but she interrupted me.

'"Boring" is exactly what I mean, thank you! Tiresome!
Repetitive! Always the same! That is boring, is it not?'
She was still glaring. 'Esmie, you must come now and try

on your dress for Holly's party! Your father has had to go to work for a few hours but he will be back soon. We must start to do your hair.'

'Why were you phoning up the lonely hearts, anyway?' Matty asked suddenly, as Juliette and I reached the door. 'Planning on finding yourself a sugar daddy, were you?'

'Matthew, do not be so … *vulgar*!' Juliette hissed, before I could even ask what a sugar daddy was. She looked at me. 'Have you told him?'

'NO!' I said, vehemently. 'And we're not going to either!'

'Told me *what*?'

'Come on, Juliette!' I said, tugging at her arm. 'It's *our* secret!' And I gave Matthew an icy look as I pulled her away.

'*Secret*?' My brother narrowed his eyes in a determined sort of a way which I should have taken as a warning sign, only I didn't.

The new dress I got for Holly's party is worth telling you about. Juliette helped me choose it. It's deep green – forest green, it says on the label – and it's got a scalloped neckline made of green lace. It's fitted above the waist and then it's all loose below with the material billowing

43

out in a sophisticated floaty sort of way when you walk. (When I showed it to Dad he said something about Marilyn Monroe and not to go standing over any air vents in the pavement.)

Juliette rejected loads of dresses before she picked this one. She wrinkled up her nose – even though she says that's something that only English people do – at the first one I tried on which was scarlet with a high ruffly neck. 'You look like a Christmas cracker!' she protested.

Then she did the same with all the other ones I tried on that were mostly bright pink or purple with loads of sparkly bits on them. 'They are so *girlish*, no?'

'Well I am a girl!' I retorted, huffily, in Marks and Spencer's because, by that time, I was starting to get tired of hiking round all the shops in town.

'Yes, and so is Holly and what will she be wearing, I wonder? A pretty little party dress with sparkles on it? I think not!' Juliette picked up a plain black dress and held it against me. 'Chic, but too old for you, I think.' She put it back and moved round to the other side of the rack.

I sighed as I dragged after her. I was beginning to know how Holly feels when she goes shopping with her father. Holly's dad is ever so fussy about Holly's clothes. He specialises in designing women's clothes himself and he's always trying them out on Holly. (He used to try them out on Holly's mum but now she won't let him.) Anyway, if Holly ever buys something from a shop then he always insists on it looking good in case anyone mistakes it for something of his.

'Holly will be wearing something very sophisticated, no?' Juliette said. 'And I will not have you going to that party like a little babyish … *doll* … just because –' She stopped abruptly.

'Because *what*, Juliette?'

She was flushing a little. 'Because you do not have a mother to help you choose nice things! OK?'

'But I *do* have nice things!' I protested.

'Huh!' She waved her hand in the air, dismissively. 'I have seen inside your wardrobe!'

'What's *wrong* with my wardrobe?' I demanded.

'All those plain trousers with the elastic in the waist!' She pulled a face. 'And those dresses with those sleeves like *this*!' She tugged at a dress nearby with puffy sleeves. 'And those funny old cardigans! Urgh!'

'My gran knitted me those cardigans!' I said, indignantly. 'And they're not old! She knitted them last year when she was stuck in the house waiting for an operation to have her cataracts removed!' My dad's mother lives in Bournemouth with my aunt. She's very old and doesn't get out much but she never seems to stop knitting things.

'Cataracts?' Juliette looked horrified. (I found out later that the word is almost the same in French.) 'See what I mean! She was blind when she made them! All your clothes, they look like they have been made by a blind person! We must get rid of them! Otherwise, what will become of you? All the other children will laugh! All the *boys* will laugh, no?'

'I don't *wear* those cardigans!' I said, defensively. 'I just keep them in case … well … in case my granny comes to stay. So I don't hurt her feelings.'

'I am the one who has feelings,' Juliette said, firmly. 'Feelings about seeing you dressed like a baby! Come, we will try that new boutique down the road.'

'But Juliette, it'll be too expensive!'

But she just waved the credit card Dad had given her in my face and told me to hurry up.

And that's how I ended up coming home with the most perfect – and most expensive – dress I'd ever owned.

'I reckon you'll have grown out of that by the time I've finished paying for it, young lady,' Dad said, as I twirled in front of him just before going out of the door. He'd seen me in my new dress before when we'd first brought it home from the shop, but now my hair was all done up in a sort of wispy French knot, and Juliette had lent me her favourite necklace to wear as well. He stretched out his hand and added, softly, 'Come here.' And he liked the way I looked a lot. I could tell.

He'd come home to run me to the party, but then he had to go back to work, though he'd promised to join us at Holly's later on. Juliette still hadn't left to go shopping and now she was standing looking at me with a big smile on her face as I stood in the middle of the hall.

Dad turned and smiled at Juliette really warmly, like he liked her as much as he liked my dress all of a sudden.

'Juliette,' I said, giving her my most angelic smile, '*please* will you come to Holly's party after you've been shopping? Just for a little while. Dad's coming, aren't you, Dad?'

Dad raised an eyebrow, looking cynical. 'It seems that if I don't, I'll be missing out on the social event of the year.'

'All the grown-ups get to have cocktails and stuff!' I told Juliette. 'Dad likes going, really!'

'Well …' Juliette smiled. 'It is true that I would be interested to meet Holly's mother.'

'Ay, yes, Holly's mother!' Dad said, letting out a snort. 'Though don't expect too many pearls of wisdom today, Juliette. After all, it is a barbecue and I guess she'll be pretty busy cooking up sausages.'

I went to jab him in the stomach because I'm fed up with the way he always makes fun of Holly's mum. He went to grab me back until Juliette started fussing that if we didn't stop mucking about, I'd crease my new dress. As Juliette started muttering in French, tugging at my dress and straightening out the waistband, Dad grinned at her. 'Would you like a hanky to spit on, so you can scrub her face as well?' he asked.

'Shut up, Dad!' I said, glaring at him. But I wasn't really annoyed. I was too busy looking forward to Holly's party.

Chapter Six

Everyone at Holly's party really liked my dress. Holly was wearing her birthday present from her father, which was clingy and fell straight down to her calves and was made of this red scrunchy material that looked like silk. It did look sophisticated but in a totally weird sort of way. Holly's mum kept telling her it was going to be all the rage in a few months' time, but even she couldn't resist adding, 'For five minutes on a catwalk somewhere at any rate.'

Fortunately Holly isn't a self-conscious sort of a person or she'd never have coped with all the looks and comments she was getting about it.

'Is your dad here?' I asked, looking around.

She shook her head. 'He couldn't make it. He's in Paris. He's going to take me there next year for my birthday. To celebrate me becoming a teenager!'

'Well don't let him talk to my dad, then. Dad thinks people should declare a state of emergency when there's a teenager in their household.'

'Is he still fighting all the time with Matthew?' Holly asked.

I nodded. 'Matthew's being a real pain at the moment.' I was about to fill her in on the details when some other guests arrived and she had to go and greet them. Lots of Holly's friends arrived with their mums and some of them had brought their dads too. I watched Holly lean against her mum who had both arms draped round Holly's shoulders. When I was younger I used to like pretending that Holly and I were sisters and that her mum was my mother too.

I hardly got to see Holly on her own for the rest of the day. Halfway through all the party games and toasting of marshmallows my dad phoned to say he wasn't going to be able to make it after all. I suddenly got into this funny mood. I get these moods sometimes. They just sort of creep up on me and it's like this big balloon inside me has suddenly popped and all the fun I've just been having suddenly seems to vanish. And I feel so bored and empty inside that I can't imagine getting any fun out of doing anything ever again.

50

I sat down on the grass and thought about how Juliette probably wasn't going to come to the party either. She was probably so busy shopping that she'd only realise she'd left it too late when the shops closed.

'Esmie, are you OK?'

I looked up. Holly's mum was standing over me with a banana wrapped in tinfoil in her hand. 'Want one of these?'

I shook my head.

She squatted down beside me on the grass and said, 'Would a hug help?'

I nodded. Holly's mum is great for hugs when I need cheering up and she never asks questions. Holly says she doesn't mind sharing her mum with me sometimes and I guess that's sort of what happens. She couldn't sit with me for very long today, though, because she had to go and see to her other guests too.

I was still sitting on my own ten minutes later, when I spotted Holly's mother speaking to a slim blonde woman who had her back to me. She was dressed in a shimmery blue dress and even from the back she looked stunning. The woman turned and I saw that it was Juliette. I couldn't believe it! She looked so different all dressed up like that! She waved and started towards me with a hot dog in one hand and a glass of wine in the other.

'Why are you sitting here on your own?' she asked, kicking off her shoes and carefully lowering herself down to sit beside me on the grass. 'I hope you haven't eaten too much. I hope you are not going to be sick.'

'I don't *feel* sick,' I said, staring admiringly at her dress.

'Holly's mother is worried because she thinks you are not enjoying yourself.' She frowned. 'Why aren't you playing with the others? You look like a little old lady sitting here all by yourself!'

'Stop being horrible!'

'I'm not being horrible! I am just caring about you. Anyway, it is very important to laugh at yourself! Otherwise you will end up with grey hair and an ulcer in your stomach from worrying too much. Now listen … I have some good news for you!' She told me that this afternoon, she'd had an idea about our Lonely Hearts Plan. 'I only thought of it when someone phoned and Matthew answered, and they thought he was your father. I thought, why doesn't *Matthew* record a message for the newspaper? He can pretend to be your father and no one will know the difference! So I asked him and he has already done it for us!'

I couldn't believe it! 'Juliette, you ... you *traitor*!' I burst out.

'But Esmie, Matthew has helped us! He has recorded a message in a deep voice sounding just like your father! I thought you would be pleased. Now we can put our advert in the paper after all.'

'I don't care! He's a stupid, nosy, big-headed, sneaky PIG!' I shouted. 'He's going to spoil everything!'

'Esmie, *calm down*!'

But I wouldn't calm down. I ranted on and on about how our Lonely Hearts Plan was ruined now and how Dad was going to end up totally single until the day he died. And how I was going to have to stay at home and look after him for the rest of my life until I went all ancient and cobwebby like that Miss Havisham in *Great Expectations*.

'*What* a catastrophe you make up!' Juliette interrupted, laughing. 'You make your life into a big disaster movie, no?'

'Well it might as well be!' I shouted. 'Nothing ever goes right for me! It's not fair!'

'Oh, Esmie ...' She made a teasing, mock-sympathy sort of noise. She does that a lot when I get sulky about things, like when I went into a mood because Matty took

53

the last strawberry cream out of the Milk Tray box when he knows they're my favourite. (It might seem trivial to her, but I *love* strawberry creams and I know Matty doesn't really and that he only takes them because they're the biggest.)

'You don't understand,' I said, in a choked voice.

'Of course not! It is such a tragic life you have, I could not hope to!'

I looked at her sharply. Juliette hadn't used sarcasm much when she first came but now she was getting pretty good at it.

'Juliette, did you *hear* what he said in the advert?' I demanded.

'No. He said he felt embarrassed to have me listening to him.'

I closed my eyes in horror.

'Esmie, I don't understand. You think what? That he has said *what*?'

I shook my head. Juliette is so amazingly naive about some things. About brothers, for a start. Juliette hasn't got any so maybe that explains it. 'You'll see,' I said, bluntly, as I stood up to go and join Holly and the others inside the house. 'You'll see.'

And one week later, she did.

Before that, though, I had to go back to school. I managed to avoid Monday by saying I felt sick after Dad had gone to work. Well, I did feel sick. I wasn't lying. I felt sick at the thought of going to French and facing Miss Murphy after what had happened last time – not to mention Billy Sanderson and his mates. And when Juliette lost her temper and shouted at me that I *had* to go to school, I ran to the bathroom and locked myself in. It wasn't my fault if she assumed I'd thrown up in there.

She felt guilty for shouting at me after that, and instead of making me go to school she phoned our doctor to make another appointment and got told that she was off sick herself.

'There's a nasty bug about at the moment,' the receptionist told her down the phone. (She's got a really loud voice so I got to hear everything she said.) 'My kids have got it too. Vomiting and diarrhoea like you wouldn't believe! If I were you I'd keep her at home until she's a hundred per cent better. You don't want her infecting all the others, do you?'

When Dad came home and heard what had happened he pointed out that I hadn't had diarrhoea – or very much vomiting come to that – and that he thought I should go back to school tomorrow and see how I felt.

Dad has got no sensitivity at all. I told him I still felt ill, and when I went to the loo he stood outside the bathroom door asking me to describe what was happening.

'Dad, go away! You're embarrassing me!' I protested.

'I don't see why. I was the one who changed your nappies, remember! *And* got you potty-trained! *And* wiped your –'

I flushed the chain so that I couldn't hear him any more, and went over to the sink. 'Dad, I've gone really pale,' I told him, frowning at my face in the bathroom mirror.

'*How* pale?' He sounded suspicious.

'Dad, this isn't a murder investigation, OK?' I snapped, switching on the yellow light above the mirror. I didn't look pale any more – I looked yellow – and my legs felt wobbly. Maybe I really was coming down with something after all.

Dad still wasn't convinced though, and the next day he drove me to school himself. I *told* him I felt sick but he just handed me a paper bag to carry around with me and promised that he'd take me straight to see *his* doctor – who wasn't off sick with a bug – if I ended up not making it through the day.

But that day and the next I actually didn't feel too

bad. We didn't have French so I didn't have to face Miss Murphy. Billy Sanderson and his mates weren't in any of my other classes and since I spent most of my breaks with Holly, hanging out in the girls' toilets trying on the make-up she'd got for her birthday, I didn't have to see them at all.

'You should just ignore them if they say anything,' Holly said, carefully applying her plum-coloured lipstick to my top lip. 'I don't know why you're getting so upset about it.'

'It's really embarrassing, that's why!' I fumed, moving so that she smudged the lipstick.

'I don't see why,' Holly said, blotting my lip with loo roll and starting again.

Holly doesn't understand things like that. She never gets embarrassed. Once she came out of the girls' toilets with her skirt caught in her knickers and everyone laughed, including loads of boys. I think I'd have died if that happened to me, but she just tugged it free and laughed herself. Nobody bothered teasing her for long because they could tell she just didn't care. Also, she's got a great memory for embarrassing things that have happened to other people at times like that. In fact, she can get pretty nasty if anyone has a go at her. Holly's a great friend when she's on your side but she's pretty scary if she doesn't like you. 'Anyway,' she said. 'What's happening with your dad? Is Juliette still trying to matchmake?'

'Sort of ...' I said. Fortunately, at that moment the bell rang so I didn't have to tell her any more.

On Thursdays – which was the next day – we have French in the afternoon, and at lunchtime I started to get this tummy ache and had to go and lie down in the school nurse's room. She was very sympathetic and sent a note to Miss Murphy explaining that I was too sick to go to French. I felt better by the time the bell rang for us to go home and I didn't tell Dad about not feeling well. I didn't give Dad the note the school nurse had given me either, because I knew he'd make a fuss and insist on taking me to the doctor.

On Friday, I felt fine. We don't have French on Fridays, and next week was half-term which meant no more school for a whole week! And then, at the end of the afternoon, Miss Murphy sent a message saying she wanted to see me first thing when we got back after the holiday. Suddenly I felt sick all over again.

'It's nerves,' Holly said, following me into the toilets after the bell had rung. 'My mum says people often feel sick when they're nervous. You should take some deep breaths and think of something nice – that's what Mum always tells *me* to do.'

So I thought about the weekend and the fact that our lonely-hearts advert was going in the paper tomorrow. But I must have been nervous about that too because as soon as I started thinking about it, the sick feeling got ten times worse!

Chapter Seven

That afternoon I got home to find Matthew in the living room being interrogated by Dad. Dad must have got home early for once. Straight away I thought he must have found out about our Lonely Hearts Plan but when I stood in the doorway to listen, I realised he had got my brother cornered about something completely different.

'So who were you with at McDonald's?' Dad sounded very stern.

'Just Jake and some guys he knows,' Matthew mumbled. He was standing facing me with his back to the fireplace, and I immediately felt like I wanted to rescue him. I don't know why I felt like that because usually I don't mind one bit when Matthew gets into trouble. Maybe it was the way his cheeks were all flushed and his fringe was standing on end and he was shuffling from one foot to the other with his hands in his pockets looking about five instead of fifteen.

'You haven't mentioned these new friends to me before.'

'Well, you've been at work all the time lately, haven't you?' Matthew said, sulkily. He paused, like he expected Dad to say something. When Dad just kept looking at him the same way, he swallowed and carried on, nervously. 'Anyway … we've all been meeting up for breakfast. Jake and me just forgot the time. We didn't mean to be late for school.'

'*Three* times in the last week, it says here.' Dad flapped the letter he was holding in front of Matthew. '*Forty-five minutes* late on one occasion.'

'It's only registration and stuff. The teachers just faff around at the start of the lessons, anyway,' Matthew mumbled, spotting me and making a rude get-lost sign at me.

I instantly got annoyed. 'My English teacher says that the first twenty minutes of every lesson is the most important because that's when you're concentrating your best!' I said, making a rude sign back.

Dad turned round at the sound of my voice. 'I would say Esmie's English teacher probably knows what she's talking about, wouldn't you?' he said, turning back to set his eyes firmly on my brother.

Matthew went all red in the face again and mumbled, 'Yes, Dad,' and I started wishing I hadn't opened my mouth. OK, so my brother's a pain, but it didn't really make me feel good to see him squirming as much as this. Our dad is pretty fair most of the time but he can come down hard on Matthew when he's done something really bad – much harder than Jake's dad ever does on him. I couldn't see Dad's face to judge how much danger my brother was really in, but I guess Matty must have thought it was quite a lot because he was hanging his head now like he expected to be grounded for the rest of the year.

'I can't believe Juliette didn't tell me about this,' Dad suddenly said.

There was silence in the room. I held in my breath. Juliette couldn't be going to get into trouble about this. It wasn't fair if Dad blamed it on her.

'It wasn't Juliette's fault, Dad,' my brother said, nervously. '*She* didn't know I was late for school.'

Dad didn't reply for a moment. Then he nodded, slowly, 'You're right, Matthew. You're a big boy and getting to school on time should be your responsibility. Now listen to me …' He pointed a finger at him. 'I accept that I've been spending too much time at work lately, but if you need me to stay at home in order to kick your backside into school for you every morning, then I promise you, I'll do it. Now, is that what you're telling me you need?'

'No, Dad,' Matthew flushed.

'Well, one more late morning and I'll start delivering you to school myself. Right up to the door of your classroom. In fact, I'll personally hand you over to your registration teacher. And I don't want you going to McDonald's every day before school. You can go with Jake once a week and that's it. Got it?'

Matty opened his mouth to protest and shut it again quickly. Even he wasn't stupid enough to start arguing again now. 'Yes, Dad,' he said, meekly.

'OK, then.' Dad put the letter back in its envelope. 'Now, you'll be pleased to know I am *not* working this weekend.'

'Can we go and see a film, then?' I asked, quickly. 'There's a new *Star Wars* film out, isn't there, Matty?'

Matthew stuck out his lower lip, sulkily, even though he'd been going on non-stop about wanting to see it ever since Jake had seen it with *his* dad last week. 'Why don't we all go on Sunday afternoon?' Dad suggested.

'Great!' I said.

Dad looked at my brother. 'Matthew?' There was a long silence while Matty deliberately kept Dad waiting for his reply. 'Matthew?' Dad said again, not sounding so patient this time.

'I *suppose*,' my brother grunted.

'Can Juliette come with us?' I asked. '*Please*, Dad.'

'I *suppose*,' Dad sighed.

'Great!' I shouted, and I raced off to ask her.

Usually I really like Friday evenings because I know that I've got two whole days of no school ahead and that I'm going to get to see more of Dad because it's the weekend. But this Friday evening was turning out to be really boring.

For starters, Juliette announced that she was going out and she wouldn't be back until late. Then at teatime, Dad asked Matthew if he'd got the marks back for his English test and Matthew yelled, 'Yes, and I failed it, OK! Shakespeare is just stupid, anyway!' And he got up and left the table, even though he hadn't finished his meal. Matthew has his GCSEs next summer and every now and then he gets really panicky about them. He especially gets panicky if he gets bad marks for stuff he's handed in.

I thought Dad would yell at him to come back, but he didn't. He sat and finished his own dinner, and made me finish mine, and then he went through to find Matty in the living room where he was lying on the sofa pretending to watch television. Dad sat down on the coffee table and started speaking to him, quietly, saying his usual stuff about how so long as Matty *tried* then that was all that mattered to him. 'Sometimes you have to persevere at things for a while before you get the hang of them,' he added, giving my brother's shoulder a gentle nudge.

Matty looked up then. 'With Shakespeare, I reckon you'd have to persevere for *ever* ... and even then you wouldn't have a clue what he was going on about!' he grunted.

Dad laughed. 'Come on. I've got some time now. Why don't we look at it together?' Dad studied English literature at university before he joined the police force, so he's pretty good at helping Matthew out if he gets stuck with it. Soon, the two of them were sitting at the kitchen table with Matty's English books spread out in front of them.

Bored, I took a KitKat upstairs with me and flopped down on my bed, wondering what to do with myself.

There was nothing I wanted to watch on television and although I had homework too, I didn't have much and I couldn't be bothered starting it now.

I looked at the photograph of my mother and started to imagine what she was thinking. I reckoned she might be thinking about us and wondering if we would ever find anyone to make us as happy as we had been when she was alive. Of course, I hadn't really been here then, except as an unborn baby, but I'm sure I must have been a very happy unborn baby with her for my mother.

'Dad's lonely-hearts advert is coming out tomorrow,' I whispered to her. 'What do you think about that?' She kept on smiling. 'Of course, he might not get any replies,' I added. 'But if he does, we're going to try and get him to meet them. I think it might be difficult, though. You know what Dad's like ...' Suddenly I had an idea. 'Maybe *you* could help?' I suggested. 'By making the right person see his ad or something. Can you do that?'

I listened hard but there was no reply, not even from inside my head.

Matty came flying into the living room the following morning with the free paper in his hand, looking like he'd just won the lottery. 'It's here! In the "Men Seeking

Women" column. Fourth from the bottom! Look! "Dishy detective with *dire daughter* seeks –"'

'*Matthew!*' I screamed at him.

He laughed. 'Only joking! Don't worry. I rewrote your stupid advert. Look … It starts with the word "singing".' He thrust the newspaper at Juliette, grinning.

'*Singing?*' I glared at Juliette. 'What did I tell you? He's changed everything!'

But Juliette had already started to read the advert out loud. '"Singing (in the bath) detective seeks soulmate to join him under the soapsuds. 43, tall, dark with hairy legs, into classical music and practising his French. GSOH essential."' She started to laugh. 'This is very good! But what is G … S … O … H …?'

'Good sense of humour,' Matty and I supplied in unison.

Matthew was looking really pleased with himself. 'Do you really think it's good?'

Juliette patted his shoulder. 'It is the best advert in the paper! We will get lots of replies from this, I think!'

I felt tears come into my eyes though I turned my head so they couldn't see. It wasn't fair! My advert had been just as good as his! 'Great!' I said, sarcastically. 'Now we're going to get some real weirdo who just wants to come round and get in the bath and start singing with Dad!'

'Come on, Esmie!' Juliette laughed. 'No more disaster stories, please! This is a funny advert! Maybe we will get some funny people answering back!'

I gritted my teeth. 'They'll be funny all right!'

'Let's listen and see if there are any messages before your father gets back,' Juliette said. Dad had just left for Sainsbury's.

'Why don't you listen to them with *Matthew*,' I snapped, 'since you seem to be doing this with him now!'

I stomped upstairs. It wasn't fair! The lonely-hearts idea had been Juliette's and mine. It had been our special secret together. And now she had let Matty take it over, as if it was *his* plan with Juliette and not mine.

On my way to my bedroom I looked into Dad's room. The upstairs phone was sitting by his bed. I paused. I had a right to hear those messages too! Ever so quietly, I tiptoed in and picked up the phone. Matthew and Juliette were already listening on the phone downstairs. So far there were four messages. Luckily you could press a button on the phone at any time if you didn't want to listen to the whole message and it beeped and moved on to the next one.

'Hello. I'm thirty. My name's Bianca. I'm a single mum. I like classical music too. I've got four kids aged –'

BEEP!

'Well, hello there! What a groovy ad! I'll get in the bath with you and your hairy legs anytime, honey, so ring me! The name's –'

BEEP!

'My name is Myfanwy ... I'm fifty. I'm single ... I sing in our church choir ... I'm five foot one inch tall ... and I'm a ... well, large woman ... I won't tell you what I weigh because I'm just starting a diet. Did I say I was single? And that –'

BEEP!

'This is Gaynor. Me and my girlfriends think you've got a very sexy voice ...' Giggle. Giggle. Heavy breathing.

'That was *my* voice, baby!' Matthew said down the phone at her.

I couldn't contain myself any longer. 'They're *weirdos*, Matthew!' I fumed at him. 'I'm going to KILL you!' I stormed downstairs to find both him and Juliette doubled up with giggles.

'They're all pathetic!' I shouted. 'If you'd put in what *I* wrote they'd be much nicer! What did you *say* in that message, anyway?' I was so busy ranting on, I didn't register Matty hurriedly putting down the phone. 'I bet you didn't say anything right about Dad! I bet you never even said what sort of person he wanted! How do you *ever* expect Dad to –'

'*Esmie*,' Juliette interrupted me, sharply. She nodded behind me.

I turned round and gasped out loud.

Dad was standing in the doorway.

'Expect Dad to *what?*' he asked. Fortunately he was immediately distracted by spotting his phone on the coffee table. 'Ah! There it is!' He walked into the room and picked it up. 'Who were you phoning?'

We all gazed at him dumbly for several seconds. Then we all started speaking at once.

'Holly!' I said.

'France!' Juliette said.

'No one!' Matthew said.

Dad stared at us. If he hadn't been suspicious before then he certainly was now. 'OK,' he demanded, briskly. 'What's going on?' He looked at the newspaper lying open by the telephone.

'Oh, we may as well tell him!' Juliette burst out impatiently.

'NO!' Matthew and I yelled together.

Juliette ignored us and picked up the paper where she pointed to the advert we had penned on Dad's behalf. 'We are trying to find you a girlfriend. See?' She shoved it under his nose.

Dad looked like he thought he must be dreaming.

'But unfortunately it has not produced anyone *normal*,' Juliette continued. 'There is still time, however.'

Dad was reading the advert now. 'Who wrote this?'

'Matthew!' I said, quickly.

My brother glared at me. 'It was your idea, Miss Smarty-pants!'

'It was not my idea! It was Juliette's idea!' I said, defensively.

'Stop arguing!' Juliette snapped. 'I don't know why you are behaving like this. It is a very good idea – an idea to be proud of! That you should care so much about your father, who has never got over the death of your mother enough to find himself anyone else – that you should do this for him!' She turned to Dad and added, 'You are not angry with them, are you?'

Dad's teeth were gritted. 'Not with *them*, Juliette, no.'

'There!' She smiled at us. 'What did I tell you? Your father is a reasonable man, is he not, despite how he seems on the surface!' And seemingly totally unaware that Dad was glaring daggers at her, she flounced out of the room.

Dad transferred his daggers to Matthew.

'Sorry, Dad,' my brother mumbled. 'It seemed like a good idea at the time.'

'We just wanted to help you!' I added, nervously. 'It's not a really terrible thing we did, is it?' I could feel tears welling up in my eyes.

Dad looked at me. 'No,' he finally sighed. 'I suppose not.'

The three of us stood in silence for a while longer.

'Dad, it's not true what Juliette said, is it?' Matthew began slowly.

'What do you mean?' Dad grunted.

'About you never getting over ...? I mean, you just haven't met anyone else, right? It's not that you *couldn't* ... you know ...' Matty swallowed.

'Matthew,' Dad replied, thoughtfully, 'I hope that one day I'll fall in love all over again. I really do.' And he walked out of the room.

'Phew!' I said, flopping down on the sofa. 'I thought he'd *kill* us if he found out!'

My brother didn't reply.

'None of those women were any good, though, were they?' I added.

72

'What women?' He looked far away.

'The women who answered Dad's advert!' I swung out my leg and kicked him. 'Wake up, Matthew!'

'Maybe only weird people answer adverts after all,' he murmured.

'We could listen again tomorrow, I suppose,' I said. 'I mean, this is only the first day. There's still time for lots more people to reply.'

But my brother didn't seem to be thinking about our Lonely Hearts Plan any more. He had gone over to look at the photograph of our mother that sits on the mantelpiece. It's a picture of her with Matthew on his fourth birthday and it was taken in our back garden. They're both wearing plastic raincoats with the hoods up. Hers is bright yellow and Matthew's is bright red. She's laughing in the picture and cuddling my brother, and you can just make out the big bump under her coat which was me. 'I wish I could remember her better,' he said, softly.

'You're lucky!' I said. 'I wish I could remember her *at all*!'

He looked at me and said, 'At least you can't miss her.'

I frowned. 'That's not true,' I said. 'I *do* miss her.'

Matthew pulled a scornful face. 'How can you miss someone you've never known?'

I didn't reply because I didn't have an answer to that. But you can miss someone you've never known. I'm certain of that. I'm certain because I always have done.

Chapter Eight

'So how come you don't have to work this weekend, Dad?' Matthew asked, as we climbed out of the car just round the corner from the cinema. It was only the three of us because Juliette hadn't wanted to come when I'd asked her.

'Yes,' I joined in. 'How come, Dad? Is it because you've caught your murderer?'

'Come on, guys,' Dad said, lightly. 'You know I'm not going to talk to you about that. Some weekends I'm needed at work and some weekends I'm not, that's all.'

'I don't see why you have to be so secretive about it,' Matthew grumbled. 'There's this boy in my class whose dad's a brain surgeon and he tells him everything about *his* job.'

'I make up stuff about Dad's job all the time,' I said. 'My dad found a severed hand yesterday ... they're just doing the fingerprints now … Guess what? There's a murderer around who's only going for Maths teachers!' I started to giggle.

Dad and Matthew were both smiling too, but they stopped abruptly when we saw the size of the cinema queue, which was curving right round the side of the building.

'I told you we should have gone to the multiplex,' Matthew said.

Dad had insisted on taking us to the old cinema on the high street because he hates the big multiscreen one on the edge of the town. This cinema only had two screens and the *Star Wars* film we wanted to see was on Screen One.

'You should have booked the seats in advance, Dad,' I told him. 'That's what Holly's mum always does.'

'You don't say,' Dad said, drily.

We had to wait in the queue for ages only to hear, just before we got to the front, that there were no more seats. 'Sorry!' the guy in the ticket office said to the people in front of us. 'You can go into Screen Two if you want. The film there is just starting.'

We looked at the poster that told you what was on. '*The Sound of Music!*' Dad exclaimed. 'Wow!'

Matty crinkled up his nose. I guessed he reckoned it wasn't very cool. Goodness knows why they were showing it, anyway, since it's been on TV so much that everyone's probably watched it by now. Not that I had, though. I'd seen bits of it but I'd never sat down and watched the whole film all the way through.

'How about it, then?' Dad asked.

I looked at my brother to see what he was going to say.

'No way!' Matty scowled.

'It's too late to drive out to the other cinema,' Dad said. 'So it's this or nothing. We can come back and see *Star Wars* next week, if you like.' He started to smile at the poster fondly like it was an old friend. 'The first time I saw this was at the cinema, with your mother!'

Matthew sighed loudly, as if Dad was suddenly the child and he was the grown-up who was giving in against his better judgement. 'Hurry up and get the tickets, then,' he murmured, gruffly. 'We're holding up the whole queue.'

Dad led the way enthusiastically into Screen Two where, bang in the middle of the screen, a young woman with short blonde hair was standing on top of a mountain, singing, 'The Hills Are Alive with the Sound of Music'.

77

Matty said, 'Jeeesus!'

'Shush!' I hissed, enthralled.

I had completely forgotten that *The Sound of Music* is all about a nun called Maria – who looks a bit like Juliette – who goes to look after the children of a widowed sea captain – who's about the same age as Dad – and ends up falling in love with him. Only neither of them realise they love each other until the horrible Baroness comes along and tries to push them apart. In fact, Maria actually *wants* the Baroness to marry the Captain at the start because she thinks it'll be nice for the children to have a mother again.

And that's when it hit me …

I mean, it was so obvious that I couldn't imagine why I hadn't thought of it before …

Dad and *Juliette* would make the perfect couple. They were just like the Captain and Maria. The Captain was really strict – just like Dad – and Maria was lots of fun and had all sorts of ideas about the children that the Captain didn't agree with – just like Juliette. The Captain and Maria had argued all the time at the beginning too, only the whole time they were arguing, they were really in love!

Well, maybe it was the same for Dad and Juliette!

Maybe they were in love too, only they just didn't realise it yet!

'Don't you think Maria looks like Juliette?' I whispered, excitedly, to Matty, as we left the cinema at the end.

'No way!' Matthew answered, screwing up his nose. Juliette is far more sexy, isn't she, Dad?'

'Pardon?' Dad looked dazed, like he hadn't quite entered the real world again after the film.

'Sexy ... Juliette is. Don't you think? I mean, can you imagine *her* as a nun?'

'Matthew ...' Dad gave my brother a warning look, and Matthew grinned.

I couldn't contain myself any longer. 'Dad?' I asked. 'Do you think real life ever turns out like *The Sound of Music*?'

My father smiled at me. 'Happily ever after, you mean? Well, I guess it has its moments.'

'But you have to *make* those moments, though, don't you Dad?' I said. That was something else Holly's mum had told me but I decided not to mention her right now.

'That's very true, Esmie,' Dad laughed, putting his arm through mine.

And I thought how it would be much easier if Dad

and Juliette fell in love than it had been for the Captain and Maria, because Juliette wasn't a nun.

I went straight home and phoned Holly to ask her what *she* thought.

'Well, it wouldn't be at all surprising if your dad did fall in love with Juliette,' Holly said, sounding extremely calm and collected about it. She went on to list all the movies she'd seen where the single father and the nanny get together.

'Yes, but do you think Juliette could ever fancy Dad?' I asked her. 'I mean, he's loads older than her!'

'Lots of younger women fancy older men,' Holly said, listing off a whole stream of famous couples where the man was twice as old as the woman. I hadn't heard of some of them but when I challenged her she had references for them all. (Mostly we were talking Holly's mother's *Hello!* magazine which Holly reads every week.)

'But Dad isn't famous,' I protested.

'Well, neither is Juliette,' said Holly. 'So that evens it out, doesn't it? Listen …' She paused to make sure she had my attention. 'In *The Sound of Music*, Maria fancies the Captain, doesn't she? And he's loads older than her!

And she only realises it when the Baroness points it out to her. So you've got to do what the Baroness did. Tell her!'

'But Maria ran back to the convent when the Baroness told her!' I pointed out in alarm. 'What if Juliette runs back to France?'

'She won't,' Holly said, firmly. 'Maria only freaked out because she was a nun, and nuns aren't meant to fall in love with *anybody*. Juliette'll be much cooler about it.'

'You think so?' I still felt sceptical.

'I'm positive. Just do it, OK? After all, what have you got to lose?'

But before I could do anything, I overheard a conversation between Dad and Juliette that made me think that maybe I *did* have something to lose – and that I should think twice before I did anything that might scare Juliette off.

It was late on Sunday night and I'd already gone to bed, but I was going back downstairs to the kitchen to fetch myself a glass of water. On the stairs I paused as I heard Dad and Juliette talking softly in the living room. The door was half open and I had a clear view of Juliette sitting on the settee with a glass of wine in her hand. I couldn't see Dad, though I could hear him, sipping a drink that was probably his own glass of wine, and talking to Juliette. He sounded sad.

'I don't know whether it's worse for a boy to grow up without a mother, or worse for a girl,' he was saying. 'Sometimes I feel Matthew seems to be taking it harder than Esmie and I wonder if it's because he actually experienced the loss of her. Whereas Esmie never knew her ... But then I worry that Esmie will need a female role model in her life more and more as she gets older. I mean, who has she really got now? Neither of her grandmothers are around that much.'

'She has Holly's mother,' Juliette said, slowly. 'And she has me.'

Dad didn't speak for a moment or two. 'She's grown very attached to you, Juliette ... so attached that I find myself ... despite all our disagreements ... hoping that you can stay in her life.'

I held in my breath. What was he saying? That he didn't want Juliette to leave? That he wanted her to remain with us as part of our family? Well, the only way for him to ensure that was to ask Juliette to marry him, just like the Captain had asked Maria ...

'I would very much like to stay in her life – and be more to her than just an au pair,' Juliette answered.

I couldn't hear what Dad said in reply to that because he mumbled it as he took another gulp of wine. As I heard him walk towards the door, I quickly slipped upstairs again so that he wouldn't know I'd been listening.

But back in my own room, I could hardly control my excitement. The two of them had been talking like people who were planning a future together. Juliette wanted to stay in my life, not as my au pair but as … what? My mother? If that was the case, then it could only mean one thing: that if Dad *did* ask her to marry him, she'd say yes!

'I listened to Dad's messages again just now,' Matthew said, when we were alone in the kitchen the following evening. 'There was a new one and she sounds pretty nice. Her name's Elizabeth.'

'Matthew, don't you think we should just forget the idea of fixing Dad up with a lonely-hearts lady?' I said, trying to sound casual about it.

Matthew grinned. 'What – because Dad and Juliette are really in love, only they don't realise it yet?'

I gasped. I'd had no idea that my brother had been thinking the same thing as me.

'I heard you on the phone to Holly the other night,' he

added, grinning. 'My sister, the matchmaker! Listen, I've got something to show you. Wait here …' He ran upstairs to his room and came down again a few minutes later with a piece of paper in his hand. 'This is the message from Elizabeth.'

'But Matthew, what about Dad and *Juliette?*' I demanded.

My brother pulled a face. 'Juliette would have to be out of her mind. I mean, Juliette's gorgeous and Dad's … well … he's *Dad*, isn't he?'

'Juliette told me she thought he was handsome,' I said, stubbornly.

'Really?' Matty shrugged. 'Well, hey … there's no accounting for some people's taste. But I still reckon this Elizabeth sounds right up his street. And she's old too – she's thirty-eight – so she's not going to worry about *him* being ancient, is she?' He waved his piece of paper at me. 'Do you want to hear what she said?' He lifted an imaginary telephone to one ear and put on a sexy female voice. *'Hello. My name's Elizabeth. I wouldn't usually answer one of these adverts but yours sounded intriguing. I speak fluent French and I love classical music. Oh, and I must confess that I have a bit of a thing about police detectives. Are you anything like Inspector Morse …?!'*

I wondered why he'd stopped and then I noticed that Dad had come into the room and was standing listening too.

'Dad,' my brother gulped, 'this lady sounds really nice. She speaks French and she likes classical music and Inspector Morse and …' He trailed off.

'Really?' Dad said, continuing to stare at him coolly. 'Well I'm sure Inspector Morse would be delighted to meet her.'

'She was probably just joking about Inspector Morse, Dad,' I put in, quickly.

'Yes,' Matthew added, nodding vigorously. 'The way she said it was really very … very *witty*. You know. *Sardonic*. Her message is still there if you want to listen to it.'

'Matthew … Esmie … I'm warning you. Stop interfering.'

'Look, I'm pinning her details to the fridge, OK?' Matthew said, adjusting our tropical fruit fridge magnets accordingly. 'You might change your mind about calling her.'

'I won't change my mind,' Dad said, firmly.

I looked at Dad, approvingly. He obviously didn't really want to meet anyone new. But just how much longer was it going to take him to realise that he'd already met the woman of his dreams?

I hoped Juliette might get jealous when we told her about Elizabeth, but instead she got all excited about her.

'She *still* doesn't seem to realise that she's really in love with Dad herself!' I told Holly. I'd already filled her in on the conversation I'd overheard the night before and Holly had agreed with me that it was better to leave them to their own devices for a bit, rather than risk scaring them both off completely. Now I was on the phone in Dad's bedroom, whispering urgently into it as I gave Holly an update on the latest developments.

'Juliette must be in an even stronger state of denial than we first realised,' Holly said, solemnly. 'She's obviously going to have to *see* your dad with another woman, before it sinks in. Maybe if she sees your dad with this Elizabeth …'

We decided that the best thing for me to do was to go back downstairs to find Juliette and Matthew and join in their scheming.

'*No way!*' was Matthew's first reaction when Juliette revealed her latest idea.

Juliette reckoned Matthew should phone Elizabeth,

putting on the same deep voice he'd used for the advert, and *pretend* to be Dad. 'She will not know the difference. All you will need to do is arrange a time and place to meet her. Then it will be simple for us to take your father there without telling him the truth until we get there. And then we just leave them together.'

'Yeah, and when Dad finds out I'm going to be toast!' Matthew protested.

'*Toast?*' Juliette looked confused as if she couldn't see what was nasty about toast. I don't think she'd grasped the bit about starting out as bread and then getting grilled.

'*Dead meat!*' I added, to clarify things.

'Pardon?' Juliette looked even more confused.

'What Esmie means, Juliette,' Matthew said, 'is that when Dad finds out he's going to commit his very own murder in *this* house and *I'm* going to be the victim!'

Juliette waved her hand at us dismissively. 'Your father will not be angry with you after he has met this Elizabeth and fallen in love with her. Unless she is horrible, of course, and he has a horrible evening with her. Then he will be angry but he will get over it!' She gave my brother a sly smile. 'Surely, Matthew, you are not so *afraid* of him as all that!'

I looked at my brother, expecting him to protest that

he wasn't afraid of Dad at all. But he just said, coolly, 'Nice try, Juliette. Listen, when Dad goes ballistic it's not gonna be your butt on the receiving end of it, is it?'

Juliette rolled her eyes in despair. 'So English,' she said, 'not to take even the slightest little risk. I mean, why try and make anything *different* happen in your life when you could have everything staying exactly the same? Matthew, you are just like your father!'

Matthew flushed. 'I'm *nothing* like Dad!'

'Like father, like son!' Juliette declared, warming up. She looked at me as if we were suddenly conspirators against Matthew. '*Esmie* is different.'

'Juliette, I am *not* like him!' Matthew snapped, his eyes flashing in anger.

Juliette shrugged. 'It is nothing to be ashamed of, to take after your father. There are worse things than being a person who conforms and does not take risks.' She smiled at me. 'You and me, Esmie, we are not so conventional. We are not like your brother, always doing the *safest* thing.'

'That's not true!' Matthew snarled. 'I do *not* always do the safest thing! I'm *always* in trouble! Esmie's the one who's always sucking up to Dad with her good-little-girl act!'

'I am not!' I kicked him on the shin.

He kicked me back, harder.

I went to grab him but Juliette got in the way. 'Stop it! I do not want you fighting! Stop it – both of you!'

'You don't know everything, Juliette!' Matthew shouted at her. 'You're not our mother, OK?! You think you're always right about us, but you're not!'

I stared at him. Why was he so upset all of a sudden?

Juliette was looking a bit surprised too. 'Even your mother would not *always* be right about you,' she said. 'All I am saying is that I do not think you are someone who likes to take risks. But maybe I am wrong?'

'Yeah – you *are* wrong!' Matthew snapped. Just watch me, OK?' And he pushed past us out of the room.

Chapter Nine

Juliette doesn't know Matthew like I do. She didn't believe he would do anything really silly just to prove his point, but I know him better than that. And what happened next made me forget all about our Lonely Hearts Plan.

Friday evening, it was just Dad and me at home. Dad had been going out to a dinner party but he'd decided to cancel at the last minute. Juliette had tried to persuade him not to, but he'd said he was too tired and that he was sick of dinner parties full of couples. He'd had a bad day at work, he said, and the last thing he needed was to have to make small talk all evening.

'He is feeling sorry for himself,' Juliette said, sounding very sympathetic, which I found confusing because I always thought that to feel sorry for yourself was a bad thing, not an endearing one. 'You must be very nice to him tonight, Esmie,' she added.

'I'm always nice to him,' I said, indignantly. 'It's Matthew who's not!' I was the only one staying in with Dad because by that time Juliette had arranged to go out dancing with one of her friends since she was no longer required to babysit and Matthew had already left for Jake's house.

Matthew was meant to be home by ten o'clock and when he still hadn't arrived by half-past, Dad phoned Jake's place and there was no reply. Dad immediately started to get jumpy, and I could tell he was worried that something had happened to him. Dad gets even more overprotective of Matthew and me when he's working on a murder case, though he never admits that to us. I think he likes *us* to think we couldn't possibly get murdered in a million years – which is difficult when he's always acting like he thinks we're going to get murdered the very next day if we don't watch out.

He sat with a mug of coffee, checking his watch and frowning as we waited for my brother to get back.

'Shall we go and look for him?' I suggested, trying to be helpful. I knew Matthew was probably just staying out late on purpose because he reckoned he needed to show Juliette that he was capable of taking risks after all, but I couldn't tell Dad that. If I did then I might get Juliette into trouble.

'I wouldn't have a clue where to look for him, Esmie –
and he knows it,' Dad said.

'You would if you'd let him have another phone,' I
pointed out. Matthew had been pretty careless with his
last two phones, leaving one on the bus a few months
after he'd got it and losing the second when he'd left it in
the changing rooms at school. Dad had been cross with
him for not looking after them better and had refused to
buy him another one. He looked like he was one regret-
ting that now.

'Knowing him, he probably wouldn't have it switched
on anyway,' Dad grunted.

'Don't worry, Dad,' I attempted to reassure him. 'He's
probably just being naughty and staying out late with his
friends. He won't have had an accident or anything.'

'An accident?' Dad said, anxiously. 'I hadn't thought
of that. The hospital would phone if he'd ended up there,
though, wouldn't they?'

'He'll be all right, Dad,' I said, going over to give him
a hug.

'Well, he won't be when *I* get hold of him,' Dad
replied, squeezing me in return.

Eventually Dad sent me to bed and I'd fallen asleep by
the time my brother finally rang. Dad came upstairs to

wake me up. It was nearly midnight and apparently Matthew had missed the last bus and didn't have any money for a taxi.

'Where is he?' I asked, sleepily.

'At a party with Jake and some others,' Dad said. 'I've told him to wait there for me to come and fetch him. Juliette isn't back yet either. Goodness knows what *she's* up to.'

Since Dad won't ever leave me in the house on my own, he made me get out of bed, put my coat on over my pyjamas and go out with him to the car. 'Why can't I just stay in the house?' I yawned, grumpily, as I slid into the back seat and lay down in order to go straight off to sleep again.

'Sit up and put your seatbelt on.' Dad sounded very tense, and I decided it was best not to complain any more.

We hadn't yet reached the community hall in town, where the party had been, when we spotted Matthew walking along the street towards us. He was all alone. 'I'll kill him!' Dad muttered, slowing down.

I started to wake up. Matty getting into trouble with Dad often has a sort of *stimulating* effect on me. I think it's because it always makes me feel very *good* in comparison.

Dad stopped the car with a jerk and leaned over to open the front passenger door. 'What the hell do you think you're playing at?'

Matthew pulled his door shut behind him. He looked wrecked. 'It's OK, Dad,' he muttered. 'Nothing's happened!'

'It's what *could* have happened!' Dad snapped. 'How *dare* you disappear off without telling me where you're going! And how *dare* you disobey me when I tell you to be home by ten o'clock!'

'We ... we sort of forgot about the time,' my brother mumbled.

Dad leaned closer and sniffed his breath. 'Have you been drinking?'

'No!'

Dad gave him a look that made him flush. Dad hates us lying to him when he's telling us off. It always gets him even angrier. 'You're grounded,' Dad said.

'No, Dad!' Matthew exclaimed. 'Look – I only had a couple of cans that Jake had with him. And I phoned you to come and get me, didn't I? Just like you're always telling me to!'

'Yes – and then you start walking home on your own instead of waiting where I told you to wait!'

'Come on, Dad!' my brother burst out. 'I could just as easily have got murdered waiting for you outside that place! Everyone else had gone home and there's an alleyway just along the side of the building that's really dark. Anyone could've been hiding in there with a knife or something!'

Dad wrestled with the gearstick in a way that made me think that my brother wasn't saying exactly the right sort of thing. 'What about your friends?' he demanded, abruptly. 'Couldn't you have asked them to wait with you?'

'And tell them what? That I was *scared*? Dad, they'd never let me hear the end of it. Besides, I *wasn't* scared ...' He glanced backwards at me and I knew he was making sure I understood that he wasn't scared of *anything*.

Dad didn't answer for a few moments. It was very quiet in the car. And then he exploded. 'Believe me, sonny, if you saw the things I have to go and see, you *would* be scared! I think, it couldn't happen to my kids! *My* kids don't walk about the streets late at night! I always know where *my* kids are! And they're sensible! They know the dangers. I've told them a million times! Oh, no,' he hissed. '*I'll* never have to go through what those families go through when some copper knocks on their door to tell them it's *their* kid's body out there!'

I sat cringing in the back seat. I'd never thought before about Dad having to go and speak to the relatives of murdered people. I tried to imagine what *I* would say if I had to go and speak to them. I couldn't even imagine what you *could* say except that you promised to catch whoever had done it before they did the same thing to somebody else. Only so far, with his latest case, Dad hadn't.

Matthew said, in a tense, tight voice, 'If you can't handle it, you should do another job.'

And that's when Dad screeched the car over to the kerb, just like they do in those detective programmes on the TV, lifted his hand and smacked him. Matthew cowered away with his arm up, as if to protect himself from what was coming next, but there wasn't anything. I couldn't see his face. Dad's breathing was heavy.

'Don't worry, Dad!' I cried out. 'You'll catch him! You'll catch him and everything will be all right.'

And you couldn't hear anything in the car after that except *me* crying.

As soon as we got home Matty went straight to his room and slammed the door.

I started to say, 'Dad –' but he interrupted me.

'Back to bed, Esmie,' he said, without looking at me. *'Now.'*

I went to bed but I didn't go to sleep. I couldn't. I think I was afraid that if I did then our family would fall apart during the night or something. I looked at my mother's photo for help but as usual she just smiled back at me as if everything was fine. I listened extra hard, but I couldn't hear her voice.

I got up and went downstairs. Dad was in the living room. I peeped inside and saw him lying back on the sofa. Then I saw him wipe his eyes as if they were damp. I wanted to go to him and tell him how much I loved him but he suddenly sat up and looked full of energy again. I darted into the kitchen so he wouldn't see me as he headed upstairs. And when I crept upstairs a few minutes later, the bathroom door was shut and I could hear him running himself a bath.

I went back inside my room and listened until the bath water stopped running. Then I heard another noise. It was coming from Matthew's room. It sounded like he was crying. Matty acts like he's really tough half the time, like he doesn't need Dad at all, but I don't think that's true really. Because whenever he and Dad have a really big row and Matty ends up being sent upstairs,

Matty gets this look on his face as if, I don't know, as if Dad's banishing him from his life for ever instead of just sending him to his room. And now that Dad had actually hit him …

If our mother was still here, she could go and give Matthew a cuddle like in that photo we've got downstairs, and then she could go and give Dad a cuddle too and everything would be all right again.

I heard a sudden noise downstairs, and for a freaky moment I actually thought my mother might have jumped right out of that photograph of her and Matthew on the mantelpiece, just because I'd wished for it. If this was a movie, that could happen. But real life isn't like the movies and when I crept out on to the landing to look, I saw that the hall light was on and Juliette was there, hanging up her coat. She was wearing her shimmery blue dress and her blonde hair was shining under the light. I waited for her to climb up the stairs and as soon as she reached the landing, I grabbed her arm.

'Why are you not in bed?' she whispered. 'What is happening?' She looked in alarm at the closed bathroom door. Dad's voice was audible now, talking quietly to himself on the other side.

I dragged Juliette into my bedroom. Quickly I told her

what Matthew had done. 'I think he did it because of what you said, Juliette,' I said, 'to prove he isn't scared to take a risk. Only Dad was really mad at him and they had a terrible row.'

'What a silly boy,' Juliette sniffed. But she looked pretty worried, just the same.

'Dad's really upset too. He's been in the bath for ages, talking to my mother,' I whispered. (Dad does that sometimes when he's worried about anything. He's a bit like me that way, I guess.)

'He is *what*?' Juliette looked like she thought I'd gone mad.

'Come and listen.' I led her back on to the landing and moved up close against the bathroom door, pressing my ear against it.

Juliette paused for a moment, then did the same. After a couple of seconds she stepped back. She looked horrified.

'It's lovely, isn't it?' I whispered, stepping back too. 'The way he still talks to her and tells her stuff. I think it's really romantic.'

'Romantic?' Juliette shuddered. 'She has been dead, how long, your mother?'

'Eleven years and seven months,' I said. Juliette already

knew that really. Dad had told her that my mother had died giving birth to me. It's not something I like to think about very much. In fact, normally, it's the one thing I never want to talk about. Somehow, though, tonight was different. Suddenly, I wanted Juliette to hear the whole story.

'She died an hour after I was born. Well, before that really, but that's when they stopped trying to resuscitate her.'

Juliette looked at me as if she knew that this was something I didn't tell most people about. 'How did it happen?'

'I don't know exactly. Dad says something went wrong that doesn't usually go wrong and they couldn't stop the bleeding. She never even got to ask if I was a boy or a girl. Dad said she wanted me to be a girl though.'

Juliette moved me gently away from the bathroom door. 'What a terrible way for him to lose her.'

'And me,' I reminded her. '*I* lost her too.'

'Of course,' she said, frowning. 'You lost her too.' She looked as if she was about to say more but instead she got distracted by the muffled sobbing noises coming from Matthew's room next door. 'Matthew is *that* upset?'

'Dad hit him.'

'But that is terrible! Your father should not be hitting him!'

'I know, but Matty was being horrible to Dad.'

'I think I had better go and see Matthew.'

'You'd better not. He hates it if people see him crying. He'll only be horrible to you too.'

Juliette shrugged. 'I was horrible too when I was a teenager. It is normal.' As she left me to go to Matthew, she paused. She turned back and said softly, 'Go to bed now, Esmie. I will see you in the morning.' Before I had time to reply, she had turned to face Matthew's door again. She knocked and even though he didn't say, 'Come in,' she went in anyway.

I tried to go to sleep but I couldn't. Not while everyone else in the house was still awake. I tossed and turned for a few minutes, but when I still continued to hear Matthew and Juliette's muffled voices in the room next door, I couldn't resist any longer.

I went and stood outside my brother's door.

'... of course he should not have hit you!' Juliette was saying. 'No matter how angry he is. No matter how tired. No matter how worried about you. He should not have hit you.'

'He stresses too much about everything! It's his own fault!'

'Well, you and Esmie are all he has. It cannot be easy being alone with no wife to support him. And when we are stressed, we make mistakes.'

'Juliette?' I pushed open the door. I didn't want to be alone any longer. I wanted to be part of this.

'Esmie, I thought you were in bed!'

'I can't sleep,' I said. 'Please can I stay for a little bit?' I screwed up my face into my most begging expression. '*Please*, Matty?'

'NO!' my brother barked.

'Wait, Matthew,' Juliette said. 'I think maybe this is important for Esmie to hear too.' She shifted to make room for me beside her on the bed even though Matthew was still scowling at me. 'Now, tell me more about this argument in the car. What did you say that made your father so angry?'

'I can't remember,' Matthew grunted.

'You said, "If you can't handle the stress, you should get another job, then, shouldn't you?"' I recounted, helpfully. 'Only you said it more nastily than that!'

'I did not!' my brother protested, flushing bright red.

'All right,' Juliette put in, quickly. 'Matthew, obviously whatever you said was very … very …' She frowned as she struggled to find the right word.

'Aggressive?' I suggested, ignoring my brother's glare.

'I was going to say *hurtful* to your father's feelings, no?'

'Dad hasn't got any feelings!' Matthew said, scornfully.

'Of course he has feelings! He just keeps them hidden most of the time. In France we tell each other how we feel and it is much better! Still … What you must do, Matthew, is tell him you are sorry and then he will tell you *he* is sorry and you can both talk about it and make friends.'

'No way!' Matthew said. 'Not after what he did!'

'Nobody *wants* to say they are sorry,' Juliette replied. 'But sometimes we must. You will have to learn that, Matthew, if you do not want to lose the people in your life that you care about.'

I was staring at her. I'd never thought before about how you could lose people you loved *without* them dying, just because you were horrible to them. That's when I noticed Dad standing in the doorway. He was in his dressing gown and his hair was sticking up where it had got wet in the bath.

'May I join the meeting?' he asked, jokily.

Matthew looked up at him and Juliette quickly stood up as if she'd been caught doing something she shouldn't. I stood up too.

'I didn't mean to hit you, Matthew,' Dad said, taking a couple of steps into the room. 'I'm sorry about that. I'd just been so worried about you. All sorts of things had been going through my head about what might have happened to you. That's why I lost it.'

My brother swallowed. He looked at Juliette, then back at Dad again. After what seemed like forever, he mumbled, 'I'm sorry too.'

We all stared at each other in silence for a few moments, and you could almost hear the house creaking.

'You're still grounded for the staying out late part, in case you were wondering,' Dad added, sounding pretty stern again. 'Don't you ever do that to me again, you hear? You want to scare me to death, or what?'

'Sorry,' Matthew muttered again, avoiding Dad's eyes.

'Come on, Esmie.' Juliette took me back to my room, leaving them together. As she watched me climb into bed, she looked deep in thought. 'I will try and think how we can get this Elizabeth and your father together, without Matthew having to do something he does not want to do.' And she kissed the top of my head and quickly left my room before I could tell her what I knew for certain now. That I wanted *her* to be my stepmother, not anybody else.

Chapter Ten

'I have been thinking about this problem of the *first contact*,' Juliette said the next morning, as she washed up the breakfast things. If Dad was the one washing up, I'd have had to dry them and put them away, but since Juliette thinks it's more hygienic to let dishes drip-dry, I was just sitting watching her.

I stared at her. *First contact?* Had I missed something? I mean, I know I'm not big on watching the news but so far as I knew the earth wasn't about to be invaded by aliens from another planet or anything.

'I have decided to make the first contact myself,' she added, holding a soapy dish under the tap. She always leaves the cold water tap running to rinse the soapsuds off each dish after she washes it, which she says is something that all French people and sophisticated English people do. Personally, I think it makes a huge mess splashing water everywhere but there's no point in arguing with Juliette when she's got a rule about something.

'How do you mean, *first contact*?' I asked, still thinking about aliens in flying saucers.

'I shall phone this Elizabeth myself!'

I gawped at her. 'You're kidding!'

'I shall do it now,' Juliette said, decisively.

'But Juliette, you can't phone her!' Why couldn't Juliette see that she and Dad would be perfect for each other, if only they'd realise it? 'What are you going to tell her, anyway? That Dad doesn't really want to meet her but we're going to trick him into it?'

'Of course I will not say that! Here! Finish these.' And she handed me the dishcloth and headed towards the fridge where she snatched off the sticker with Elizabeth's phone number on it.

Juliette! You can't!' I gasped, dripping soapy water all over the floor as I followed her out to the hall where she picked up the telephone to dial the number. I tried to grab the phone but she pushed me away.

'Hello?' she said, and I could feel my heart pounding. She grinned at me. 'Perfect. It is the answering machine.' Then she listened for a few more seconds and started to speak into it. 'Hello, is that Elizabeth? I have been asked

to give you a message by my boss, Detective Inspector …'
She paused and began again. 'Sorry! I am meant to say
that this is a message from *the singing detective*.' She
paused again, more dramatically. 'He has been trying to
get in touch with you but could not get through. He has
booked a table for lunch tomorrow – Sunday. This is at
the new French restaurant near the town hall. You know
it? He is sorry not to be able to speak to you directly but
he could not get through before and now he has been
called away today with his work and he does not know
when he will get the chance to phone again. He thought
he might not have written down the right number for
you. I think it is just that he cannot read his own writing!
I can hardly read his writing! He says if lunch tomorrow
is not convenient you can phone him at home tonight.
His number at home is –'

'Juliette!' I hissed, making a second attempt to snatch
the phone away from her, but she carried on, giving our
number apart from the last digit which she gave as six
when it's really zero.

I stared at her. Was she mad?

'The table is booked for one o'clock and he says he
will meet you in the reception area of the restaurant.
Thank you. Goodbye.' And she put down the phone.

'Juliette, are you crazy?' I nearly shouted at her. 'Dad hasn't booked any restaurant – and that's not even our phone number – and –'

'I have everything under control,' she interrupted me. 'I will book the table and then all we have to do is persuade your father to take you there for lunch tomorrow. That shouldn't be difficult as he will still be feeling guilty for what happened with Matthew. And since I will tell him they are having a special French-speaking day at this restaurant tomorrow and it will be very good for you and Matthew to practise your French, I think he will agree, no?'

'But it's meant to be a *date*!' I protested. 'She isn't expecting me and Matthew to turn up too!'

'No, but as you walk in the door, you and Matthew will spot her and you will tell your father what we have done. He will be too embarrassed to leave her standing there and he will have to speak to her. You and Matthew can come back home and leave them. If she is nice, then your father will get on with her and all will be well!' She smiled super-confidently.

'Juliette, it'll never work!' I protested. 'Dad'll kill us if we do that! And anyway, what if she doesn't turn up?'

'Then we have no problem. We just say that I must have been mistaken about the French-speaking lunch.'

'Well, what if she phones him back?'

'Ah, but she cannot. I have made a mistake with reading your father's handwriting. His zero, it looks like a six, no?' She was so pleased with herself, she looked like she could go floating up to the ceiling at any minute, just like Mary Poppins.

I just gaped at her. She was incredible! And that's when I completely flipped.

'Juliette *why* are you doing this?' I shouted at her. 'Why are you doing this when you and Dad could get together and then everything would be *perfect*?!'

'Pard*on*?' She said it the French way with the emphasis on the end bit, looking as if she thought she must have misunderstood me.

'You and Dad would be great together, Juliette,' I said, grabbing her by the arm. 'You have to stop this lonely-hearts thing. It's just silly. Dad doesn't want to meet anyone that way and I don't want him to either. I want him to get together with *you*!'

'Esmie, are you serious?' Juliette's expression was one of complete disbelief, as if I'd just suggested she get together with King Kong. '*Me* and your father? You are really thinking this?'

'Yes, Juliette!' I replied, enthusiastically.

'But, Esmie ...' She was gaping at me now. 'I do not like him in that way!'

'Maria didn't realise she loved the Captain until the Baroness told her she did!' I said. 'You just have to give it a chance!'

'*Maria*? The *Baroness*? Esmie, what is wrong with you?' She frowned and peered suspiciously at my eyeballs as if she thought I might be on drugs or something.

'It was in *The Sound of Music*,' I explained. 'You know! That film we saw about the nun who goes to look after the children and ends up falling in love with their father. Maria looked just like you – except you're not a nun! And Holly says lots of women marry men who are much older than them! Actresses sometimes marry men who are old enough to be their *grandfathers*. Holly saw this wedding in *Hello!* magazine where –'

'Esmie, I am *not* marrying anybody's grandfather, OK?' Juliette sounded impatient now. 'I don't know why you would think this. Does your father know that you have this ridiculous idea in your head? Because if he finds out he will not be pleased! And I am not pleased, either!'

'Dad likes *you*, Juliette,' I said, stubbornly.

'Rubbish! I can tell if a man likes me in that way.

Anyway, I have a new boyfriend now. I met him when I was out dancing last week.'

I felt like I'd been slapped. 'You can't have.' My lip was beginning to tremble.

'His name is Peter. He is English but he is very hand-some. He is taking me out on a date next weekend.'

I stared at her. I couldn't speak. How could she do this to Dad? How could she do this to *me*? How could she start acting like a mother and making me get to love her and then tell me she was going off to be with someone called Peter instead of with us?

'Esmie ...' Juliette put her hand on my arm but I pushed it away roughly.

'*I hate you!*' I screamed at her, and I ran upstairs away from her as fast as I could.

I lay on my back on my bed and held my mother's photo in my hand. I really stared at it, looking for any details I hadn't seen before. Her eyes looked happy as they looked at whoever was taking the picture. I realised now that I'd never asked Dad anything about the day that photo was taken. I didn't know whether he was the one who had taken it or what they were doing in the countryside that day or anything like that. The photograph had been in my bedroom for as long as I could remember and I'd never seen any other copies of it. I don't think I'd ever thought before about it being just a snapshot of my mother's life like all the other pictures of her in the numerous photo albums we had. I'd always thought of this particular photograph as sort of ... I don't know ... sort of *containing* my mother, I suppose. Once, when I was much younger, I'd taken the frame apart and looked in the back of it almost expecting to find her there. When we were little, we'd had a nanny who read *The Lion, the Witch and the Wardrobe* to me, and instead of imagining the backs of wardrobes opening up into strange magical lands, I had started to imagine opening up the back of my mother's photograph and being able to jump inside it into *her* land, wherever that was. But when I'd opened up the back there hadn't even been a scrap of paper with a message from her inside. If I was writing a storybook, that's what I'd make happen. I'd make my heroine open up a photograph of a person who was missing and she'd find a secret message from them there and then she'd be able to go and find them.

My mother looked young in the photograph. Dad told me once that it had been taken even before Matthew was born. My mother was wearing a white shirt and blue jeans and she was leaning against a gate with a field stretching out behind her. I thought about how Juliette never wears white because she doesn't think it's a very flattering colour. Well, she was wrong. She was wrong about lots of other things too, like how cats are cleverer than dogs, and how salads are meant to be eaten at the end of a meal, not on your plate with everything else.

'Esmie ...' There was a gentle knock on my door.

'Go away,' I called out.

My door opened anyway and Juliette walked in.

'Haven't you ever heard of *privacy*?' I hissed at her. I wanted to say something really mean, and it wasn't until she'd come all the way over and sat down beside me on my bed that I thought of something. 'Or don't they have that in stupid old France?'

'You are angry with me, not with France, I think,' Juliette said, looking down at me solemnly.

'I'm not angry,' I said, turning on to my side so I didn't have to look at her.

She put one hand on my leg. 'Come on, Esmie. You are very angry!'

'No, I'm not, so just *shove off*!'

'See what I mean?'

'Go back to your precious France! I don't care. I think France is stupid anyway, the way you all sit around eating cheese all day and ...' I stopped because she had started to laugh. I pulled my legs up and twisted round so that I was sitting up on the bed. 'I wish you'd never come here! And why did you tell Dad you wanted to be more to me than just an au pair, if you didn't mean it?'

She stopped laughing then. She looked puzzled at first, then she realised what I was talking about. 'You were listening to our conversation the other night?' When I didn't reply, she continued speaking anyway. 'Esmie, I am sorry I have upset you. What I meant was that I hope that you and I can still be *friends* long after I stop being your au pair.' She paused, looking at me more closely. 'Esmie, if I was much older or something, who knows ... maybe then I would have romantic feelings for your father. But right now, to me, he seems a bit like *my* father. Can you understand that?'

I frowned. '*Your* father?'

She nodded. '*My* father is only a little older than yours.'

'Really?' Somehow I hadn't thought of Juliette having a father of her own back in France, especially not one who was anything like mine.

She nodded. 'Yes. We argued a lot when I lived at home. He was very strict with me when I was a teenager.' She smiled. 'He said he thought I needed it. We argued even more than Matthew and your dad. You should have heard us!'

'*I* don't argue very much with Dad,' I said, because suddenly it seemed really important to prove that Juliette and I – and our fathers – were very different.

'No,' Juliette said. 'You don't. But you might when you get older. You are his little girl now and he is happy with that. But fathers sometimes find it difficult to watch their little girls grow up and leave them.'

'I won't ever leave Dad,' I said, fiercely. 'When I grow up and get married, he can come and live with me if he wants to.'

Juliette didn't say anything. She picked up my mother's photo instead, which I'd left lying on the bed. 'She is very pretty in this picture, your mother. She would have been, what …? Forty-one … forty-two, maybe … if she was still alive now?'

'Yes, but that doesn't mean Dad *only* wants to be with someone the same age as him!' I protested, because you didn't have to be a genius to work out what she was leading up to.

'Have you asked him?'

'Of course not!'

'Well, maybe you should. Esmie, I would really like you *not* to think of me as ...' She frowned. 'I am only eleven years older than you. Your father, he is *twenty* years older than me! Esmie, I do not want to be *anyone's* mother yet! I do not want to have children myself for a very long time. I want to go out to parties with my friends and go travelling and have some nice boyfriends and just have lots of fun! I will not be ready to settle down for a long time. Can you understand that?'

I stared at her. I'd never thought before about Juliette actually being closer in age to me than to Dad, and closer to me in the things she liked to do, as well.

'Esmie, listen. I want you to go and see what this Elizabeth is like tomorrow. You don't have to like her. But I think you should not make up your mind until you meet her. Remember, the object is to get your father dating again, and *not* making a mess of it. So you have to give this Elizabeth a chance, for his sake. Just a *chance*, OK? Will you do that?'

'Dad probably won't like her anyway,' I said, stubbornly. 'So what's the point?'

'The point,' Juliette said, firmly, 'is for you to learn *not*

117

to decide your father's love life for him, before he has had a chance to decide it for himself.'

I gaped at her in disbelief. I mean, I reckoned that was pretty rich, coming from her!

Chapter Eleven

The following morning, Juliette told Dad about the new French restaurant and their special French-speaking Sunday lunch. 'You must take the children there today!' she said. 'I will book you a table!'

'I don't think so, Juliette,' Dad murmured, without looking up from his newspaper. 'I've got a few things I need to do.'

We were seated at the kitchen table eating our separate breakfasts. Dad was eating toast and marmalade; I had just shaken out a very large bowl of crunchy nut cornflakes; Juliette was drinking coffee because she never eats breakfast and Matthew was hanging over the toaster, waiting for his toast to pop up.

'But Sunday is a family day,' Juliette said, firmly. 'You should not be working.' She gave me a sharp nudge.

'Yes, Dad,' I began. 'Holly's mum says one day a

week should always be set aside to spend with your family!'

Juliette glared at me. I don't know why. I was doing my bit like she wanted, wasn't I?

Dad looked up. 'Holly's mum,' he began, sounding irritated, 'doesn't have a job that means she has to *work* at weekends.'

'But, Esmie, you would very much like to go out to lunch with your father today, wouldn't you?' Juliette prompted me.

'Oh, yes!' I said, quickly. 'Please, Dad. Can we go to this French place today? I really want to practise my French for school!'

'Swot!' Matthew said, from behind me.

'Shut up!' I snapped, and we were about to start arguing when Dad switched on the radio. It was the local radio station and they were talking about Dad's murder case. I could tell it was his case immediately by the way Dad stopped chewing his toast. The news broadcasters were describing it as an investigation that didn't seem to be going anywhere fast and they were quoting the victim's uncle as saying he reckoned the police weren't using enough sniffer dogs.

I started to ask Dad how many sniffer dogs they *were*

using when Juliette suddenly said, 'Esmie,' and gave me a warning look.

But no warning look of Juliette's was going to stop Matty launching into *his* views on how murder investigations ought to be conducted, which involved cutting down on manpower and employing more computers instead. According to Matty, computers are less likely to cave in under public pressure and arrest the wrong person like the police are always doing.

I could tell Dad was annoyed because he piled two spoonfuls of sugar into his coffee instead of one. (He's been trying to cut down.) Then he glared at my brother. 'Listen, young man –' he began, which is always a bad sign.

And then Juliette intervened. 'Come,' she said, soothingly to our father. 'He is fifteen, no? You must not take him seriously. At his age he has too many ... you know ...' She waved her arms up and down searching for the word she wanted.

'Spots?' I suggested, helpfully.

She frowned. 'No, no. I mean the things that make the spots!' Juliette's English is not at its best first thing in the morning.

'Grease?' I offered, ignoring my brother's angry scowl.

121

'I think you mean "hormones",' Dad said, starting to laugh as he put out his arm to stop Matthew from thumping me.

'*Oui!* And too many of these means he thinks he knows everything, no?' Juliette said.

'*Oui!*' I sang out, ducking as Matthew chucked the lid of the marmalade at me.

'I'm going out!' he hissed, slamming his plate into the sink even though he hadn't even used it yet.

'Wait!' Dad got up and turned off the radio. I thought he was going to remind Matthew that he was still grounded but instead, he smiled at him. 'Perhaps I do need to forget about my work today! Juliette,' he said, and she looked at him, 'I think this Sunday lunch is a good idea after all. Would you like to join us?'

Juliette beamed. 'Oh, no thank you. I have other plans. But I am sure you and the children will have a lovely time. I'll book a table for one o'clock, shall I?'

And she winked at me as she glided past the fridge where Elizabeth's details were still clamped to the door.

Juliette didn't really have other plans, of course. Her only plan was to wait at home until Matthew and I returned so that she could look after me while Dad continued on his date. It was pretty nice of her, really, considering that Sunday is meant to be her day off.

Matthew refused to come with us at first. He pointed out that if he was meant to be grounded, then he couldn't, but Dad said that he was giving him a break for good behaviour. I knew my brother was still in a bad mood about the way we'd all ganged up on him at breakfast. I think Dad was trying to coax him out of it because he started up some conversation about how long women always take in the bathroom and how men are much quicker even though they have to shave.

'Matty doesn't need to shave!' I said, but this time Dad took Matthew's side.

'We'll have no more big-brother baiting this morning, thank you, Esmie,' he said, firmly. So I had to shut up, and me having to shut up seemed to improve Matthew's mood no end, because after that he agreed to come with us.

The new French restaurant was on the high street, a little way along from the town hall. I started to worry that Elizabeth wouldn't find it but Matty said that since there were no other restaurants in town called *Le Nouveau Restaurant Français*, he didn't see how she could miss it. When we'd told Matthew the real reason we were going there to lunch he said he reckoned it was going to be a right laugh getting a look at Elizabeth so long as I realised that *he* wasn't going to be the one to tell Dad who she was when we got there.

Which meant I was going to have to do it – *if* Elizabeth turned up. After all, maybe she wouldn't respond to the message Juliette had left. I wasn't sure if I really wanted her to or not, now. If Juliette and Dad were never going to get together – and now it was beginning to seem like they really weren't – then I suppose I did want some sort of stepmother. But only if she was just as nice as Juliette, and I really didn't see how she could be.

'I can't believe I'm doing this,' Matthew kept saying, sniggering so loudly that I was sure Dad was going to notice and get suspicious. 'I just hope she's here. You realise if she's not, we're going to have to sit through some boring lunch, with Dad making us speak French to all the waiters.'

'Shut up!' I snapped. I was getting so nervous that I started to definitely hope Elizabeth *wouldn't* be there as we approached the restaurant. I looked anxiously at my watch. It was nearly a quarter past one. 'We're late, Dad,' I said, tensely.

But he had already opened the door to go inside.

In the little waiting area there was a huge French family with loads of kids running around. Dad immediately rubbed his hands together and looked pleased. He started going on about how this restaurant must be good if real French people were choosing to eat in it when they could just as easily eat proper French cooking at home.

I looked around. I couldn't see any single ladies standing around looking like they were here on a blind date.

'If you'd like to just wait here, Sir, we will have your table ready shortly,' the French man behind the desk told us. He had an accent just like Juliette's.

'When do we have to stop speaking English?' Dad asked him, jovially, but all he got in reply was a strange look.

At that moment a lady came out of the little door with *Mesdames* written on it. She was on her own. I stared at her, holding in my breath. So did Matty.

Dad was peering at the nearby fish tank. 'I haven't had lobster in years,' he said, pointing at something black and huge with claws that was sitting amongst the weedy stuff at the bottom. 'Look, Esmie. How do you fancy having one of those for your lunch?'

I didn't reply. I was too busy scrutinising the lady who was now leaning against the wall opposite us. If it was her, then she was different from how I'd imagined her. I couldn't really think how I *had* imagined her except that I'd had a vague idea that she might look a bit like the Baroness in *The Sound of Music*. She didn't, though. The Baroness had blonde hair but this lady had dark hair like my mother. She had on a cream cotton dress with a loose reddish-brown jacket over the top and she kept pulling the jacket closed like she was trying to disappear inside it. The front door opened and she looked towards it nervously, but when a couple walked in arm-in-arm, she seemed to relax. Was it her?

'Matty, did she say what she looked like in that message?' I whispered.

''Fraid not,' he teased. 'God, I'm going to die of embarrassment if you ask her. There isn't anyone here we know, is there?'

But I didn't ask her. I just kept staring at her, trying to make up my mind if she was here to meet Dad or not, and if she was, whether I really wanted her to.

Suddenly, she rushed into the toilets again.

I told Dad I needed to go too. I don't know what I was expecting to find her doing inside. I guess it was silly to expect her to pull the lonely-hearts column out of her bag and wave it around just to oblige me. In fact, she was standing in front of the mirror tugging at her hair, which was tied up in a sort of loose bun which she now seemed to be trying to dislodge. She caught me staring and smiled at me. I thought how the Baroness had smiled at the children in *The Sound of Music* while she was dating the Captain at the start, when all the time she was planning on sending them away to boarding school. Juliette would never send me away to boarding school. But then, Juliette wasn't an option now, was she?

I quickly dodged into the nearest cubicle and waited until I heard her go out. Then, after a few more minutes, I went back outside too. The French family had been taken to their table now. Dad and Matty were still waiting in front of the lobster tank. So was she, and she was checking her watch again. I ignored Matty as he pulled a face at me.

'Nobody seems to be speaking French here,' Dad said, when I joined them.

'Maybe Juliette made a mistake,' I said.

'I wouldn't put it past her. Excuse me,' he said to the woman, 'you wouldn't know if this is the day they're having the French-speaking lunch?'

I nearly fainted. He wasn't meant to be talking to his date *before* we had established who she was.

She smiled at him. 'Sorry – not that I know of.'

I looked at my brother to see if he recognised her voice but he was too busy trying not to laugh.

'Our table seems to be taking a long time,' Dad added, conversationally. 'Have you been waiting long as well?'

'Well, I'm actually waiting for someone else,' she replied, glancing at the door again as it opened, but it was only one of the waiters coming back inside from a break. She looked at her watch as the head waiter came over and asked her, very loudly, what name her table was booked under.

'Well …' she muttered. 'I don't know, actually.'

'What is the name of your friend?'

'I'm afraid I don't know,' she floundered. 'His surname I mean.'

'Perhaps he has booked under his first name?' the waiter persisted. 'Some people do.'

'Oh, no,' she said. 'I don't think so. I think I may have made a mistake about the place. It's all right. I'll just wait a little longer and if my friend doesn't come, I won't need a table, thank you.'

My brother was doubled up now trying not to laugh out loud. Any minute now I was going to thump him.

'Excuse me, but would you like to borrow my mobile to call your friend?' Dad suddenly asked her. Like I said before, Dad can never resist coming to the aid of a damsel in distress.

'Thank you, but I don't think …' She gave an embarrassed little laugh. 'I think I may just have to accept graciously that I've been stood up!'

'Surely not –' Dad began, but the waiter interrupted him.

'Your table is ready now, Sir. The booking was made for *two* people … but I take it you would like us to lay another place?'

'Oh, right, was it?' Dad gave him an apologetic look. 'I don't know how that happened, but yes, we'll need it for three. Come on, kids!' He gave our mystery lady a smile. 'Hope he turns up!' Then he started to follow the waiter.

'Ask her,' my brother mouthed, giving me a little push before following Dad.

I waited behind but at the last minute I couldn't do it. I just went bright red and found that I couldn't say anything at all. I left her standing there and rushed to sit down with my father and brother.

Matthew rolled his eyes as I pulled in my chair. 'Scaredy cat!'

Dad looked up from his menu. 'What are you talking about?'

'Nothing!' Matty said. 'Dad, can I have a beer?'

'No, you cannot,' Dad said, frowning.

'Jake's dad lets *him* drink alcohol,' Matthew complained.

'Perhaps Jake's dad and Holly's mum should get together and write an instruction book for other parents,' Dad replied, crisply.

Matthew shut up. He knows when to sometimes, thank goodness.

I noticed that Dad was still watching what was happening over at the reception area. The waiter was talking to the lady who was still standing there. She seemed to be getting ready to leave, though.

I took a deep breath. I had to do something, otherwise all our planning would have been for nothing. 'Dad –' I began.

But Dad didn't hear me. He seemed totally distracted with his own thoughts. 'Wait here a minute,' he muttered, and he stood up and strode back across the room himself.

Matthew and I stared at each other. What was he *doing*?

We saw him speaking to the woman. Then they both spoke to the waiter. All I could think was that they must know after all. Juliette must have told Dad or something.

But if that was it, then why hadn't Dad said anything before?

'I don't believe it!' Matthew murmured, as the two of them started to walk back together towards our table. 'He's asked her *himself*!'

'But he *can't* know!' I said. I felt giddy, almost as if the room was spinning.

'Maybe he doesn't. Maybe he just fancies her and he's decided to try his luck.' My brother gave a low whistle. 'Way to go, Dad!'

I couldn't believe Matthew was being so calm about it. The whole thing was crazy. Really spooky. It was like our plan was being taken over by … well … by some psychic force or something.

Dad reached our table and pulled out the spare seat for her. He took her jacket as the waiter laid out an extra place. 'If your friend arrives, feel free to join him, of course,' he said, as he handed her his copy of the menu.

She shook her head. Her hair had red streaks in it, I noticed. It wasn't the same colour as my mother's at all. 'I wouldn't dream of it,' she replied. 'No, if he arrives now then he can just … well … go away again!' And she laughed. She had a nice laugh, like she really meant it and wasn't just laughing to be polite.

'Don't introduce us, will you, Dad?' Matthew said, cheekily.

Dad ignored him. He was speaking to his guest, giving her his full attention. 'I remember something similar happening to me once. I'd arranged to meet someone in a very posh restaurant and she didn't show up. I was mortified! But it turned out she was waiting for me at a different place. We found each other, eventually. Well, she ended up marrying me ...' And he smiled as he pointed to my brother and me. 'This is my son, Matthew, and my daughter, Esmie.' Apparently he had already told her *his* name. I remembered that we hadn't actually said it in the advert, which was just as well.

'Matthew ... Esmie ... I'm very pleased to meet you,' she said, beaming at us. 'I'm Lizzie. Lizzie Watson.' And she held out her hand.

Chapter Twelve

Fortunately, the waiter took so long to come for our order that Dad got up from his seat to go and call him.

'Is Lizzie short for *Elizabeth*?' I asked her, the second Dad was out of earshot. Matthew was staring at her like she was on display in a zoo or something and I just hoped he stopped before Dad got back.

Thankfully she didn't seem to notice Matthew gawping as she smiled at me and nodded. 'But I tend to only use my full name in formal situations. This isn't a formal situation, is it?'

'Oh, no!' Then, because I didn't know what else to say, I added, 'Dad's pretty strict about table manners, though.'

'Well I'll just have to be on my best behaviour, then, won't I?' she replied, laughing.

'Oh, I didn't mean *you*!' I said, quickly. It was funny

but I still didn't feel like she and our mysterious Elizabeth were the same person at all.

She smiled. 'Now *your* name is really pretty. It's French, isn't it?'

'No,' Matthew answered, before I could stop him. 'It's short for Esmerelda. After our great-aunt! Esmerelda hates anyone to call her that, though, don't you, Esmerelda?'

I kicked him under the table and he was kicking me back when Lizzie said, 'My favourite children's book, when I was little, was about a Princess Esmerelda. I think it's a wonderful name!'

'Really?' I was pleased and I gave my brother a superior look.

'What did Princess Esmerelda do, then?' Matthew sneered. 'Go around snogging lots of frogs?' And he started to laugh in a really loud, dirty sounding way, which made a lady at the next table turn and look at him.

I glared at him and Lizzie looked like she was wondering whether or not to say something, then smiled in relief as she spotted Dad returning with the waiter.

Dad put his hand on Matthew's shoulder as he came up behind him, which made my brother stop abruptly in mid-snigger. 'Is this OK, Lizzie?' Dad nodded towards the bottle of red wine the waiter was carrying.

Lizzie beamed. 'Lovely. But let me get the wine. Oh, and my share of the meal, of course …' And then they both started getting all embarrassed as they argued about who was paying. Honestly, if they'd known the whole truth about this lunch thing they'd realise they had a lot more to worry about than that.

'So, Lizzie,' Dad asked, filling both their glasses again after we had finally ordered. 'Do you live locally?' Dad was sitting opposite her and had hardly been able to tear his eyes off her face for long enough to look at his menu. He was downing his wine very rapidly, I noticed, and I wished he'd stop. His face was going all pink and having a pink face was bad according to a survey I'd read in *marie claire* (which said that eight out of ten women prefer men who don't blush).

'Yes,' she replied. 'And you?'

'Just across the other side of the park,' Dad answered. 'It's just the three of us,' he added, quickly. 'I'm a widower.'

'It's *not* just the three of us,' I reminded him. 'There's Juliette too.'

'Juliette?' Lizzie asked, taking a sip of wine very slowly.

'Oh – she's just our au pair,' Dad said quickly.

For some reason Matty seemed to find that funny. I don't know why because it really annoyed me. After all,

Juliette wasn't *just* anything. 'She's almost like part of the family, really,' I said, loudly.

Dad pressed his finger on a drip of red wine that was running down the outside of his glass. 'Juliette and Esmie are quite close,' he said. 'Close in age too, really. Juliette is hardly more than a teenager herself.'

'She's not! She's twenty-two!' I said, indignantly.

'Juliette's always trying to get Dad matched up with someone because she reckons he's been single for long enough,' Matthew put in quickly. 'Isn't she, Ez?'

I looked across at my brother suspiciously. It was unlike him to start saying things that were in any way helpful. 'Are *you* single, Lizzie?' Matty added, grinning.

'Matthew, don't be so rude!' Dad said, sharply.

'It's OK,' Lizzie half-smiled. 'Yes, Matthew. I am, as a matter of fact. Are *you*?'

'Of course he is!' I said. 'No one in their right mind would go out with *him*!'

'I don't know about that, Esmie,' Dad said, lightly. 'Don't look now but I just saw the girl at that table by the door having a good look at him.'

Matty and I both turned to look at once and Dad laughed. The girl he was talking about had long blonde hair and looked about Matty's age. She glanced across at us as if she could feel us staring, then quickly jerked her head back again to say something to her parents.

'Maybe she thinks you look cute,' I teased my brother. 'Holly does – well, she thinks your bum does, anyhow.'

'Shut up, Esmie,' Matthew said, flushing bright red as Lizzie smiled and Dad looked ... I don't know ... just really happy and relaxed for a change.

Dad took another gulp of wine and started to ask Lizzie more about herself. Gradually they got more and more animated, as if they were really enjoying each other's company. I wished they'd stop drinking their wine so fast, though. I didn't want each of them thinking that the other one was an alcoholic. I couldn't believe how nice Lizzie was turning out to be. I was dying to go home and tell Juliette all about her, and then Lizzie asked what Dad did for a living.

I nearly choked on my lemonade. I should have known this was too good to be true. As soon as Dad told her he was a detective, she'd realise he was the same man as the one in the advert she'd answered. And then everything was going to go up in smoke!

'Dad's a pharmacist!' I announced, quickly.

Dad stared at me as if I'd gone mad. So did Matty.

But Lizzie said, excitedly, 'I don't believe it! So am I! I work in the chemist next to the bus station.' She knocked her glass as she lifted it and some wine splashed on to her dress. 'Oh, no! Hang on a minute!' She dashed off to the ladies' to wipe it off.

As soon as she'd gone, Dad turned on me, looking furious. 'Esmie, what do you think you're doing?'

'Well, you're always telling people you're a pharmacist when we're on holiday,' I said, weakly.

'Duh-uh,' Matty sneered, like I was really thick. He grinned wickedly at Dad. 'Hey, it's a bit of a bummer, her actually being one, isn't it? I mean, you don't know much about drugs and stuff, do you, Dad?'

'Don't be silly! I'll tell her the truth, of course, as soon as she gets back,' Dad grunted, crossly.

'Dad, I don't think you should do that …' I began, trailing off because I couldn't think how to explain everything without ruining things even more.

As soon as Lizzie got back to our table – with a big wet splodge on her dress now instead of a wine stain – she started talking very rapidly herself. Her face was very flushed and some more of her hair had fallen out of its knot. 'Do you know, I feel I must tell you something … I am really glad that you're a pharmacist and not a … well …' She smiled. 'A *police detective*, for example!'

I just about fell off my chair. So did Dad. 'A … *police detective?*' he stammered.

'The man I was meant to be meeting here is one,' she went on. 'It was a blind date to tell you the truth, and I don't actually *want* to meet him now! I've been out with a policeman before and he was so *bossy*! Oh, no, I never want to have anything to do with policemen ever again!' And she beamed at Dad as if she'd just shifted a huge weight off her shoulders.

Dad looked like he wanted to sink through the floor.

Matthew started to make funny snorting noises into his napkin.

I said, 'What? Not *ever?*' at which point my brother burst out laughing and had to excuse himself from the table.

'I … see …' Dad stammered. Frantically, I signalled to him to keep quiet but he ignored me and carried on doggedly. 'Well, in that case, Lizzie, there's something I'd better tell you …'

You'll never believe what happened next. Dad told her the truth about his job and she didn't mind! It turned out her father had been a policeman as well as her horrible ex-boyfriend and because of her father, she'd always thought that policemen were lovely and that's why she'd always wanted to go out with one in the first place. Only her ex-boyfriend had turned out to be not very lovely at all. She went on about her father then, about how he'd been such a good policeman and such a great dad and how she really missed him because he'd died a few years ago. I thought she should make up her mind. I mean, either she hated policemen or she didn't. It all got a bit boring after that and you'd think Matty and me weren't even there, the way Dad and Lizzie were ignoring us. Still, at least she didn't seem to have clicked that Dad was the same policeman as the one whose advert she'd answered.

At the end of the meal, Dad invited her back for coffee, and I was pleased.

It wasn't until we were all walking home together that I remembered. Juliette didn't know that everything hadn't gone according to plan.

As soon as we got home, I rushed all around the house looking for her but I couldn't find her anywhere. Maybe she'd gone out.

'We could have coffee in the garden if you like,' Dad

was saying, when I got back downstairs. He had taken Lizzie into the kitchen and was gesturing for her to sit down while he put the kettle on. Matthew, who was stuffing his hand inside the biscuit barrel as if he hadn't just eaten a huge Sunday lunch, said he was going round to Jake's, and Dad said, 'I beg your pardon? You're still grounded, remember? Rest of the weekend.' Matthew stomped off upstairs in a huff and Dad raised his eyebrows at Lizzie and said, 'Got any kids?'

I don't know why but I felt really pleased when she shook her head. I didn't know whether I should hang about in the kitchen or leave them to it, but then Lizzie started to ask me about school and what class I was in and what my favourite subjects were and I sort of got the feeling that she wanted me to stay. She would make a really good stepmother, I decided. She didn't talk down to me like some grown-ups do and she really concentrated when she was listening to my opinions, even though my opinions tend to go on a bit.

Dad was just pouring out the drinks when the back door opened and Juliette walked in from the garden holding a book and an empty mug. She beamed as soon as she saw Lizzie. 'Juliette, this is –' Dad began.

'I know, and this is *wonderful*!' Juliette interrupted,

rushing up to Lizzie and kissing her on both cheeks like she was an old friend. 'So it went well, then, the lunch? I am *so* pleased.' She turned to me. 'Didn't I tell you it would all work out! Are you not proud of your father?'

Dad was staring at her like he thought she must have got too much sun. I didn't dare look at Lizzie.

'Juliette, I need to speak to you,' I growled. 'In *private*!' And I jerked my head for her to follow me into the living room. '*Now!*'

As we left the kitchen, Dad said to Lizzie, 'You couldn't turn round and grab the milk out of the fridge, could you?'

And that's when I remembered.

'NO!' I shouted, diving back in to the kitchen again. But Lizzie was already standing staring at the sticky note pinned to our fridge door – the one with her name and telephone number on it.

Dad saw her looking and said, cheerfully, 'That's a phone number I won't be needing now – you can throw it in the bin if you like!'

Lizzie turned and gaped at Dad as if he had just turned into a completely different person.

'What's wrong?' he asked, setting down the jug of coffee.

'How did you get this?' she demanded. Her voice was trembling slightly.

'Pardon?' He looked puzzled.

'This is really ...' Lizzie's voice dried up and she shuddered. She started to back away from Dad, very slowly, as if she was trying not to give way to panic. 'How did you know my number?' she repeated, hoarsely.

'*Your* number?' Dad said, shaking his head. 'No, no, that's –'

'Lizzie!' I called out, desperately. 'It's all right! We can explain ...'

But from the way she bolted out through our front door, I could tell that the only thing she thought I was about to explain was that Dad was some weirdo stalker axe-murderer and Juliette and I were his accomplices!

Chapter Thirteen

OK, so now you know. Never listen to your au pair when she comes up with some hare-brained scheme to try and matchmake your father.

Dad really started doing his police detective stuff after Lizzie left. He told Juliette he wanted to speak to me and Matthew on our own, then he got my brother downstairs and interrogated the two of us together until he'd found out everything. Then he told us both to go to our rooms.

'You should not blame them,' Juliette said, rushing in as soon as Dad had opened the living room door to let us out. Juliette pointed out that if he wanted to blame someone, he should blame *her*, and he yelled that he *did* blame her. And then they had the most terrible argument you can possibly imagine. Matthew and I could hear them shouting at each other as we sat together on the landing. Then Juliette slammed the front door and left.

She came back again but she and Dad have hardly spoken to each other since, and when I tried to talk to Juliette about what had happened, she kept changing the subject. And I didn't dare ask Dad anything.

I was sure Juliette was going to leave, and over the next few days I found myself sitting in school worrying that she'd have gone by the time I got home. Then, on Thursday, Miss Murphy asked me to stay behind after class so she could talk to me – *again*. I'd already been to see her straight after half-term like she'd asked me to and told her I didn't have a problem with French. I don't think she believed me but she couldn't say anything else because I was attending all my classes now and when she'd tentatively mentioned what had happened that day with the advert, I'd acted dead cool about it. I *felt* pretty cool about it too. I found that I didn't care any more what she or any of the stupid kids in my class thought about my dad. I mean, if they wanted to think he was a complete plonker who could only get a date through an advert in the newspaper, then so what?

The bell had gone and everyone else was filing out of the classroom. French was our last lesson. I looked across at Holly who shrugged and mouthed that she'd wait for me outside the doorway.

Miss Murphy waited until all the others had left. My heart was starting to beat faster. What had I done wrong now? It was true I'd been pretty distracted at school over the last few days and hadn't been giving much thought to learning French or anything else. I hadn't finished any of the exercises we'd been set and I'd stopped putting up my hand all the time to ask questions like I normally do. I'd stopped answering Miss Murphy's questions too, when she wanted responses from the class. I mean, what was the point in showing off my French now that Juliette was leaving?

'Esmie, is something wrong?' She was right beside me now.

'No, Miss.' I avoided her gaze, focusing on doing up the zip on my schoolbag.

'Well, perhaps you could tell me if you're planning on doing any work ever again in my class or if you've gone on strike for good?'

I swallowed. Miss Murphy can be pretty scary if you get on the wrong side of her. 'Sorry, Miss.' I started to edge towards the door.

'Esmie, are you normally in the habit of walking away while people are talking to you?'

I stopped edging. 'Sorry.'

'For heaven's sake, would you stop saying sorry and tell me what the matter is?' Miss Murphy burst out. 'You've been abnormally quiet in class since you came back after half-term. I haven't had to tell you off for talking once and that's not like you at all!'

Unfortunately Holly chose that moment to emerge from the doorway and answer for me. 'She's just upset because her dad's mad at her, Miss.'

'Shut up, Holly!' I snapped.

Holly gave Miss Murphy a look like they were two grown-ups together. 'Esmie tried to fix her dad up on a blind date and it went a bit wrong,' she added.

'HOLLY – SHUT UP!' I bawled, pushing her aside and racing out of the classroom.

In the girls' toilets I burst into tears. How dare Holly tell Miss Murphy about Dad! I wished I'd never told her what had happened now. I might have known she'd go around telling everybody.

Someone was knocking very gently on the door of the toilet.

'Esmie, are you in there?' It was Miss Murphy.

I pushed open the door and my reflection glared back at me from the huge mirror on the opposite wall. I looked pretty deranged. My hair was a tangled mess, my eyes were red and teary and my face was all puffy and ugly.

'Oh, Esmie!' Miss Murphy gushed, pulling me out of the toilet cubicle and squeezing me against her huge bosom so that she nearly suffocated me. Holly said afterwards that it was a good thing we'd been practising how to hold our breath under the water in swimming, or I'd have been asphyxiated for sure.

'Don't you think it would help if Esmie talked about it, Miss?' Holly chipped in, from the doorway. 'My mum says you should always talk about things that are worrying you.'

'Well, yes ... I'm sure it would ...' Miss Murphy stammered, awkwardly letting go of me.

'I told you, Esmie!' Holly said, triumphantly. 'You'll feel much better if you tell it all to Miss Murphy! Won't she, Miss?'

Miss Murphy didn't say anything. She just stood there looking ... well ... at her watch, actually. Like I said before, normally I'm known as a bit of a chatterbox.

Miss Murphy took me into her office and sent Holly home – which Holly didn't appreciate at all – and I ended up telling her just about everything. I didn't tell her how much I loved Juliette and how I'd really wanted her and Dad to get together, but I told her all about our Lonely Hearts Plan and meeting Lizzie and how that had all gone wrong. And then I told her what had happened after Dad found out. And when I got to the bit about Dad saying all those horrible things to Juliette and the two of them arguing and Dad still being so angry that I was sure Juliette was going to leave if he didn't calm down soon, I started to sob all over again.

'All right, Esmie, let's think about this for a minute,' Miss Murphy said, swiftly handing me a box of tissues. 'Now would it help, do you think, if we knew *why* your father is so angry?'

'It's because of what Juliette did, of course. And me – only he blames her more than me because she's a grown-up.'

'Yes, but is that the whole reason? It's part of it, yes. But I wonder … It sounds as if your dad and this lady were getting on rather well.' She had a twinkle in her eye. 'I wonder if your dad wasn't more upset about losing that opportunity than anything else!'

I stared at her. Dad had been getting on well with Lizzie, definitely. But if that was what he was most upset about – Lizzie walking out on him – then why was he taking it out on us? It didn't make sense.

'Now …' Miss Murphy was looking at her watch. 'We really should leave before the caretaker locks us in! And won't they be wondering where you are at home?'

'Probably,' I said, shrugging like I didn't care if they were.

'Oh, Esmie,' she sighed, as she led the way downstairs and out to the teachers' car park. 'Come on. I'll give you a lift, and that should get you home a bit quicker.'

I expected her car to be all prim and proper just like her, but it was full of sweetie wrappers and other bits of rubbish. The back seat was piled high with books and papers and the sort of stuff you'd expect in a teacher's car but there was also a baby seat. I stared at it. I'd always imagined Miss Murphy sitting at home every evening all alone with her glasses on her nose, reading some long complicated book in French. I looked around her car a bit more. There was a toy rabbit on the floor and a pair of kiddie's shoes. On the back ledge there was a tub of baby wipes.

'Have you got a *baby*, Miss?' I asked, twisting round to look at her. Suddenly she didn't seem nearly so familiar.

She nodded. 'Danny – he's two. I have to collect him

from the childminder in five minutes but it's in the same direction as your house so I should get there in time.' She smiled at me.

I couldn't believe it! No wonder she'd been looking at her watch.

'Miss Murphy ...' I wanted to say thank you but I felt like maybe that would be breaking some sort of rule. Somehow teachers weren't people you usually thanked for doing stuff for you.

'It's such a pity,' Miss Murphy said, suddenly, 'that *someone* couldn't go and see this Lizzie and explain what happened. You never know, she might even be persuaded to give it another go.'

'There's no way she'd give it another go!' I burst out. 'She thinks Dad is Count Dracula or something!'

Miss Murphy laughed. 'Still ... people can surprise you.'

And as she stopped the car in front of my house I had to admit that *she* had certainly surprised *me*.

I got home that evening to find Juliette cooking a huge dinner. Juliette cooked everything using her mother's recipes in what she called the proper French way. As far as I could tell, the proper French way just consisted of calling things fancy French names rather than English ones but I didn't dare say that to Juliette. I was just really glad that she was still here. Instead of tomato soup we were having *soupe à la tomate* and instead of carrot salad we were having *salade de carottes*. There was some very red-looking meat and lots of different cheeses too.

'Your father phoned to say he will be home late,' she told me, when I asked where he was. 'I thought we would have dinner without him – a nice dinner because it is my birthday today.'

'Your birthday!' I exclaimed, horrified because I hadn't got her anything. Not that it was my fault! I mean, she hadn't told me.

'Yes, I am twenty-three today,' she said, smiling. 'And I need cheering up so I have been cooking all day!'

'Why do you need cheering up?' I asked her.

'Because I am not in France with all my friends and family.'

I stared at her because it had never occurred to me that she missed her home. She hardly ever talked about it except when she was telling us how much better France was than England. 'Don't you like being here with us any more?' I asked in a small voice.

She came over and hugged me. 'I love being here with

152

you, Esmie. I wish I could take you home with me! But the rest – it has been difficult, no?'

'What about your boyfriend?' I asked her. 'I thought you really liked him.'

She frowned. 'Peter has decided he does not want me for his girlfriend after all. He told me yesterday.'

'Oh, no! I'm sorry, Juliette!' And I really did feel sorry that she was unhappy. I was longing to cheer her up so I said, 'I'm going to go out right now and buy you a birthday present!'

'Don't be silly. Help me set the table instead.'

I shook my head. 'Matty can do that. I'm going to get you something for your birthday.' And I rushed upstairs to find my purse.

I went down the road to the shops and bought her a bunch of flowers and a big bar of Belgian chocolate. I couldn't find any French chocolate but I figured that at least I hadn't bought English. When I got back Matthew still wasn't home and Juliette said we may as well start without him. She was just serving up when the door slammed and my brother came in, looking very pleased with himself. I immediately saw why.

'What do you think, then?' he said, grinning.

'Dad's going to kill you!' I said. At least he'd got the

stud in his ear and not in his nose, but still. Dad had told Matthew ages ago that he wasn't allowed to get any part of his body pierced until he left school.

Juliette rolled her eyes upwards. 'I might have known there would be no peace in this house even on my birth-day,' she sighed.

'It's your birthday?' Matty exclaimed, and getting his ear pierced must have done something to his brain because he started singing 'Happy Birthday To You' in a daft mixture of French and English.

'Matty, *why*?' I whispered to him when he'd stopped horsing around. What I meant was why annoy Dad *now* after everything that had just happened? Why make things even worse?

'Because I'm fed up with him throwing his weight around all the time!' Matty said, crossly. 'He needs to know that he's not the boss in everything no matter how much he shouts at us.

We were all in the kitchen doing the dishes when Dad arrived home. I immediately went quiet and Matty tensed up too. Only Juliette kept chattering normally. We told Dad it was her birthday and he was grudgingly wishing her many happy returns when he noticed Matthew's ear and stopped talking.

'Is that *pierced?*' he asked, sharply.

'Yeah,' Matthew said.

'And you didn't think to discuss it with me first?'

'*So?*'

'*So* … you can take it out right now!' Dad snapped. '*Then* you can ask me what I think. *Then* I'll think about whether I'm going to let you put it back in or not.'

'I can't take it out. I've got to keep it in all the time at the beginning or else the hole will close over,' Matty said, defiantly.

'Tough. Go upstairs and take it out now, before I really lose my temper!'

'No, Dad, I'm not going to, and you can't make me!' Matty looked really white-faced now but I could see he wasn't anywhere near backing down. I felt scared. He'd never talked back to Dad like this before. What was going to happen?

'Matthew …' Dad was walking towards him with a look on his face like he was going to take the earring out himself.

But Juliette interrupted. 'For goodness' sake!' she gasped, throwing down her dishtowel and making to leave the room.

Quick as lightning, Dad whirled round on her. 'I

suppose *you* think this is all right, do you? I suppose *you* think I should let my children do exactly what they like and not bother about it?'

'I would not dream of contradicting you in front of the children,' Juliette said, stiffly, walking out into the hall.

'All right, then! Let's hear what you've got to say *without* the children!' Dad snarled, and he followed behind her, invited her to step into the living room with him, and slammed the door.

Matthew and I looked at each other in alarm. 'Come on,' Matty whispered.

We crept into the hall and put our ears against the closed living room door where their voices were just loud enough for us to hear.

'I only mean that you should save your arguments for things that really matter,' Juliette was saying. 'I mean, if Matthew wants to experiment with things and if it's not doing anyone any harm, then why not let him? You can't say no to everything! If you do, then he won't listen to you when it's something really important.'

Dad's voice was taut. 'Juliette, I am *sick* of you interfering in my family. Ever since you got here you've done nothing but tell me how to bring up my children … and how many kids have *you* brought up, by the way?'

'None,' Juliette replied. She paused. 'You know, it is probably just as well that you stay single. You could never let a woman be properly involved in your family. She would have her own ideas and you … you would find them too threatening. You would always tell her how you brought up your children all these years on your own, so you don't need her help now, thank you! And it would be true! And so she would leave them alone, and they would think she didn't care about them and you would have total control and you would not be a proper family at all.'

Matty and I gawped at each other. We'd never heard anyone say things like that to Dad before. And suddenly I had this crazy thought: if this was *The Sound of Music*, this is where Dad would admit that he was completely wrong and start singing to Juliette about how much he loved her.

But he didn't.

Instead, he exploded. 'You're sacked, Juliette! Do you hear me? I want you out of my house by this time next week!'

'He can't do that!' I cried out to Matthew. 'He can't!'

But Juliette seemed to half-expect it because she said nothing. She came out of the room as Matthew pulled me back hurriedly into the kitchen. We stood silently watching as she walked in her most dignified manner across the hall and up the stairs. And Dad didn't follow her, or call her back, or tell her not to go, because this was real life and in any case, he wasn't in love with her.

I started to tremble.

Matthew had tears in his eyes. 'I wish I'd never got this stupid thing,' he said, gritting his teeth as he yanked the earstud out of his ear and threw it on the floor.

'What are we going to do?' I whispered, trying to keep my voice steady.

'Something,' he said. His face was all screwed up. 'We're not just gonna let this happen. Come on. Let's go up to my room.'

And I knew then that Matthew must be feeling really terrible because he hadn't *invited* me into his bedroom in years.

Chapter Fourteen

I hadn't even realised that Matthew liked Juliette so much.

'So what are we going to do?' I asked again, sitting down next to him on his bed. He didn't answer but just kept staring into space. I started to look round his room. He had a photograph of our mother on top of the table where he did his homework. Unlike the one in my room, it hadn't been taken before he was born. He was with her in the photograph, being held on her hip while she grinned at the camera. 'Matty, do you ever think that having Juliette is a bit like having a mum?' I asked him. 'More than the other au pairs, I mean ... I mean, they used to pick us up from school and do the house-work and play with us and stuff but I never really felt like they ...' I trailed off.

'Juliette's not old enough to be our mother,' Matthew snapped.

'I know, but it still feels different with her than with the others,' I insisted.

'They didn't stand up to Dad the way Juliette does,' Matthew said. 'That's the difference. They didn't get so *involved*.' He looked unusually thoughtful. 'You know, when Juliette came into my room that night, it was weird.' For a moment I thought he wasn't going to say anything else. Then he started talking again, very slowly. 'There was this time when I was little … about four, maybe … I remember crying in my room. I was in trouble for something. Can't remember what. Anyway, I was in my room crying and I remember *her* …' He glanced at our mother's photograph. '… coming in. She said, if you tell Daddy you're sorry, everything will be better. I always remember her saying that to me.' He shrugged. 'I guess Juliette coming in that night felt like … Well … I guess it did remind me a bit of Mummy.'

I did a double take. I'd never heard him call our mother that before. I'd never even thought how he must have called her that before she died. In his mind, she was still the same as when he was little, whereas I didn't have her in my mind at all. Not the real person. I only had *my* mother – the one I talk to – but she wasn't here with me the way our mother had once been here with Matthew.

But Juliette was here. She was a real person. And I didn't want Juliette to become a distant memory. I wanted her to stay in my life for ever. I *loved* her. Why couldn't Dad see that? Why did he have to send her away?

'I hate Dad!' I said, bitterly. 'I wish *he* was dead and not our mum!'

'You shouldn't say that,' my brother said.

'I don't care,' I said, stubbornly.

'Well you should,' Matthew said, frowning. 'Because I used to wish *you* were the one who'd died and not my mother, and Dad always defended *you.*'

'You wished *I* had died instead of her?' I felt like he'd kicked me in the stomach.

'I was only little,' he said, looking at me steadily. 'Dad explained to me that it wasn't your fault she died, but sometimes I'd blame you just the same.'

I didn't know what to say. My head felt muzzy.

'Don't worry,' Matthew added, giving my shoulder a playful nudge. 'I started to love you in the end. I didn't have much choice. I got into so much trouble for trying to smother you in your cot that I had to give up!'

'I'm sorry,' I said, smiling a little.

'Sorry for what?'

'Sorry for saying that about Dad,' I sniffed. 'But Matty, we've got to stop Juliette from leaving! What are we going to do?'

And that's when I remembered my conversation with Miss Murphy.

The next day Matty and I met up after school. Usually Matthew likes to pretend he doesn't even know me in school, and today he wanted me to wait for him at the bus stop rather than directly outside the school gate. I suppose he was worried his friends might not think he was very cool if they saw him hanging out with his little sister.

We caught a bus to the bus station. Our plan was to find the shop where Lizzie worked and go and speak to her. As the bus turned into the road that led to the station, we scanned the shops on each side looking for the chemist's and went over again what we were going to say when we got there.

'What if she yells at us?' I said. 'Or what if she won't speak to us at all?'

'Whatever happens, it'll be over soon in any case,' Matthew said, firmly. 'Anyway, what have we got to lose?'

It was true. The only thing we had to lose was Juliette, who was going to leave in one week's time if we didn't do something fast.

We were just climbing off the bus when someone yelled out my brother's name and we looked across to see two teenage boys hanging out by the station shop. Matthew waved to them.

'Who are they?' I asked.

'A couple of the guys from McDonald's.'

'Hey there, Matt! Who's your girlfriend?' one of them called out, and I immediately disliked him. He had ginger hair and he looked a couple of years older than my brother.

'Come on, Matthew. We've got to find Lizzie,' I reminded him, tugging on his jacket.

'Esmie, go and wait over there, OK?' He tried to shove me in the direction of the bus station exit while he went to greet his friends, but I followed behind him.

'Hey, Matt. Guess what? Your pal, Jake, is breaking the law as we speak,' the boy with ginger hair said, grinning as he lit up a cigarette.

'What d'you mean?' Matthew started looking round to spot Jake. 'He wasn't in school. I thought he was off sick.'

'Nah! We were just hanging out. Teaching Jake how to get himself some freebies from the shops.'

Matthew looked surprised. 'What? Nicking stuff, you mean?'

'He didn't reckon he had it in him. But we knew he did really! Hey! Way to go, Jake!' We looked across and saw Jake emerging from the shop. He had both hands inside his pockets. He looked surprised and a bit embarrassed when he saw Matthew and me standing there.

'Here you are,' Jake said, pulling a couple of CDs out of his pockets. 'What are *you* doing here?' he asked my brother.

'Jake, did you really *steal* those?' I asked, wide-eyed. I couldn't believe it. Nobody I knew stole things.

'Shut up, Esmie,' Matthew said, quickly.

'Jake tells us you're not allowed out for breakfast any more, Matt,' the ginger-haired boy said. 'Too scared of your dad or something. That's what you said, wasn't it, Jake?'

'I'm *not* scared of him,' Matthew said, glaring sideways at Jake, who was looking a bit sheepish.

'Prove it then. Go and nick us something else!'

'Don't Matty!' I said, frightened. It was wrong to steal.

Dad never even told us that any more. He just assumed we knew it.

'Little sister's ordering you about now, Matt,' the ginger one grinned. 'Don't tell me you're scared of her too! Go and grab her some sweeties or something. That'll shut her up!'

Matthew put his arm round my shoulder, protectively, which surprised me. 'I don't do anything just because someone tells me to,' he said, stiffly, glaring at the ginger one. 'Come on, Esmie.' He started to turn me away from them.

'That's not what I heard. I heard your old man's really got you under his thumb. *Yes, Daddy! No, Daddy! Three bags full, Daddy!*' he mimicked, nastily.

And that's when Matthew pushed me out of the way, turned back and went for him. The ginger guy let out a yell and hit him back, and then the two of them were punching and shoving each other while Jake and the other guy tried to pull them apart.

'Stop it!' I screamed out. I was terrified. I'd never seen my brother fighting before. I was scared he'd get killed or knocked unconscious or arrested if he didn't stop. As Jake pulled my brother away and the other boy held on to the ginger one, I got in between them. My brother had a cut on his cheek and blood coming out of his nose. The ginger guy's right eye was all swollen. They were both breathing really heavily.

'Take him home, Esmie,' Jake said, as he let go of my brother and started to back away. 'We're getting out of here. I'll ring you later, Matty, OK?' And he went off with the others while Matthew held his hand up to his face and stared after him with a funny look in his eyes, as if he'd expected him to stay with us, not go off with them.

'Are you all right?' I asked him, gently, reaching up to touch his cut cheek. Matty and Jake had been best friends for as long as I could remember. 'Shall I go and phone Dad?'

'Don't be daft. Come on.' He started to walk away.

'Where are we going?'

'Where d'you think, dummy? To find Lizzie.'

We walked along the road in silence. Matthew was holding his arm like it was hurting him but I didn't dare ask him again if he was all right. I wished Dad was here. Or Juliette. I didn't really want to go and face Lizzie right now but Matthew seemed determined to carry on as if nothing had happened.

Inside the chemist's, there was a young woman behind the till. We went over to the main counter, and I waited for Matthew to say something but instead he started fumbling amongst the cough sweets. I could just make out the top of somebody's head in the back behind the screen that separated the shop from the dispensing area. I couldn't tell if it was Lizzie or not.

'Can I help you?' the young woman asked, suspiciously, staring at the drying blood on my brother's face as if she thought he might be about to start a fight in here as well.

'We need to speak to the pharmacist,' Matty said, too loudly. He sounded so nervous and he was acting so strangely, I was sure the woman would think this was some sort of hold-up. But just as I was imagining her pressing the secret button under the counter and summoning the entire local police force, including our father, to the rescue, the pharmacist came out front – and it was Lizzie.

'Goodness,' she said, looking horrified as she saw my brother. 'You look like you've been in the wars.'

And to my utter amazement, Matthew started crying.

Lizzie rushed round to sit Matthew down on one of the seats where people waited for their prescriptions. Then she started telling the girl at the till to fetch some cotton wool and some warm water. I watched her gently cleaning off the blood from my brother's face and got this funny feeling inside. I felt like I wasn't me, but somebody else, watching all this from a long way away. And just as I was feeling pleased that we had found Lizzie again, I started to feel really scared as well. Because what was she going to say when we told her why we'd come?

Lizzie had plenty to say. She had an idea too, which she wanted us to take back to Dad. We wanted her to come home with us to see him tonight, but she said that wouldn't be giving *him* the choice about whether or not he wanted to see *her* again. We had to do it her way, or not at all, she said. So we agreed to give her way a try.

Juliette had just gone out when we got back, and Dad looked in a better mood for a change. Before we could tell him about going to see Lizzie, he wanted to know what had happened to Matty. He insisted on taking off the plaster Lizzie had put on Matthew's cheek in order to survey the damage for himself. Lizzie had cleaned up his face so he didn't look so bad but he still had a swollen lip and his cheek was quite puffy too. Dad got a packet of frozen peas out of our freezer and told Matthew to hold it against his face, then he wanted to know everything.

'Matty was in a fight but it wasn't his fault,' I said, quickly, when my brother didn't reply.

'It wasn't a proper fight,' Matthew muttered. 'It was just this mate of Jake's.'

'I don't see how Jake can still *be* his mate!' I said, hotly. 'Anyway, Jake shouldn't have –'

'That's *Jake's* problem,' Matthew interrupted, giving me a quick, *button-up* glance.

'Have you and Jake fallen out?' Dad asked, gently pushing Matthew's fringe back off his face in a way I hadn't see him do in ages. Matthew didn't move or say anything but his eyes sort of went all hurt-looking. 'Oh, dear.' Dad put his arm round my brother's shoulders and gave them a squeeze. 'Come on. Jake and you have been friends for a long time. I'm sure you'll sort this one out.' He kept his hand on my brother's shoulder as he added, 'So do you want to tell me what you were fighting about?'

My brother sniffed. 'Not really.' He gave me a sideways glance to let me know that I wasn't to say anything either. I didn't see what the big deal was, since I reckoned Dad would be pleased, not angry, if he knew Matthew had refused to go and steal stuff with Jake and the others. I guess Matthew didn't want to tell in case Dad phoned up Jake's parents and got him into trouble – which he deserved, in my opinion.

'Where were you, anyway?' Dad asked. 'And why was Esmie with you?'

'We were at the bus station,' Matthew said. 'Dad, there's something we need to tell you –'

Just then, Dad's phone rang and he answered it immediately in his work voice. I hate his phone sometimes, I really do. It always rings just when I don't want it to. I'd like to throw it down the toilet or something, only Dad says that if I ever do, he'll throw *me* down the toilet after it.

'Why can't your work ever leave you alone?' I fumed, as he told the caller he'd ring back in two minutes. 'It's not fair!'

'Esmie, I always have to be available when there's a murder investigation running. You know that. They might just want to keep me informed about something. It doesn't mean I'll have to go in.' He took his phone upstairs to return the call in private. He always talks where we can't hear him if it's anything to do with work.

Matty and I waited in silence until he came hurrying back downstairs. He usually doesn't say much about his work but yesterday he'd let slip that they'd taken someone in for questioning. That often means they're about to make an arrest. And if they make an arrest that means they've caught their murderer – unless they've arrested the wrong person, of course.

'Got to go, I'm afraid,' Dad said, looking pretty keyed up about something. 'Now what was it you wanted to tell me?'

Matthew shook his head. 'It can wait.'

'OK. Tell me tomorrow. Matthew, you'll have to stay home and look after your sister.' He picked up his car keys, which were lying on top of the newspaper on the table. 'Oh, and I want you to record something for me. It's a programme on … Now, where is it?' He picked up a pen and the TV guide, and marked whatever it was on the page. 'Juliette is staying over at a friend's, so don't expect her back, and I don't want you waiting up for me either. I don't know how long this is going to take.'

'What's up, Dad?' Matty asked. 'Won't your suspect talk? Have you got to *beat* a confession out of him?'

Dad rolled up the TV guide and swatted him on the head with it. 'I'll deal with you later, sunshine.' He disappeared through the door, calling back, 'And don't think I don't know exactly how many beers there are in that fridge!'

'We'll just have to wait until tomorrow morning to tell him,' I sighed, as we heard his car pull out of the driveway.

'I don't believe this,' Matty exclaimed.

'What?'

He was looking up the thing Dad had asked us to record. 'This programme. It's called *Au pairs from Hell*!' He shook his head at me. 'How are we *ever* going to persuade him to let Juliette stay?'

'We will if we get him and Lizzie back together,' I said, frowning. 'He'll be happy then and he won't be angry with Juliette any more.'

'Esmie, even if Dad does agree to meet Lizzie again, it doesn't mean they're going to hit it off,' my brother warned me.

'I know that!' I replied, impatiently.

'And even if they do, and Dad does ask Juliette to stay, that doesn't mean she definitely will. I reckon she's pretty cheesed off with him. She might be only too glad to head off back to France.'

'We've just got to try, that's all,' I murmured.

My brother seemed about to say something else but he must have thought better of it because he closed his mouth again and went through to set the Skybox for Dad.

I set my own alarm for the following morning because I didn't trust Matty not to sleep through his. At nine o'clock I went into my brother's room to wake him up like we'd agreed.

He yawned as he sat up in bed and pushed his hair out of his eyes. He was bare-chested and his chest didn't have a single hair on it, unlike Dad's. I didn't think Holly would think he looked so adorable if she could see him this morning, though I had to admit his face had got better looking since Dad had taken him to the doctor to get some stuff for his spots.

'Come on. It's time,' I said.

Our plan was that I would wake Dad up with a tray of tea and toast and tell him what Lizzie had said when we'd been to see her the day before.

'He's more likely to listen to you,' my brother had reasoned, when we'd been deciding who should tell him. 'Especially if you put on your Daddy's-little-girl act.'

So after we'd made Dad's breakfast, Matthew carried the tray upstairs and handed it to me outside his door. He gave me a thumbs-up sign and whispered, 'Good luck,' as I went into Dad's room.

Dad was snoring when I went in. I carefully set down the tray on the end of his bed.

'Dad?' I shook him and he rolled over, nearly sending the whole tray flying. 'Dad, I've made you breakfast in bed.'

He started to rub his eyes. 'Hey!' he grunted.

'I've made you breakfast in bed,' I said again. 'To say sorry. For what we did.'

'Huh?' He looked like he was having trouble keeping his eyes open as he heaved himself up and pushed back his pillows to lean against them.

'We're really sorry we set you up on that blind date with Lizzie. We didn't think it would all go wrong like that,' I continued, quickly.

Dad looked more awake. 'Hmm ... Well ... Knowing Juliette, I expect she made it sound like it couldn't possibly go wrong!' he said. Then he sighed. 'All right, I forgive you. Come here and give me a kiss, then!'

I shrieked as he pulled me towards him because Dad's kisses first thing in the morning are horrible. It means him rubbing my face with his scratchy chin and it always really tickles. But at least he didn't seem mad at me any more. I didn't want to spoil things so I waited until he'd finished all his toast before I said, slowly, 'Dad, can I ask you something?'

'Of course, sweetheart!'

'Did you really like Elizabeth ... Lizzie, I mean ... when we were all together in that restaurant?'

Dad put his teacup down. 'Well ... yes. Didn't you?'

'Yes, and I don't blame her for leaving like that when she saw her phone number pinned to our fridge!' I said. 'She must have got a terrible fright!'

'Well, of course she must!' Dad frowned. 'I'm surprised she didn't report me to the police! I did phone her the next day to try and explain but her number was disconnected.'

'You *did*?' I sat up. This was news to me.

He nodded. 'She obviously didn't want to speak to me again.' He frowned again. 'It was a really irresponsible thing that Juliette did! It wasn't harmless at all!'

'Dad ...' I began slowly, 'if I told you Matty and I had been to see Lizzie and told her everything and that she wasn't mad at you any more, what would you say?'

He stared at me.

'We went to see her,' I added, quickly. 'At the chemist. We told her what happened. She was OK about it. Well, not at first, but she was after we'd talked for a bit.'

'Esmie –'

'We thought she'd be less freaked out if she knew the truth,' I continued, rapidly. 'And Dad, she's not freaked out at all now. And she said she wouldn't mind meeting you again if you really wanted to. Please, will you meet her again, Dad? She's going to be in the park this morning walking her dog – well, her aunt's dog. Dad, you don't have to go right this minute,' I added in alarm, as he pushed his tray away and swung his legs round very rapidly. 'She won't *be* there until eleven o'clock. She said she always sits for a bit by the duck-pond …'

'Esmie, I am getting up in order to use the bathroom,' Dad interrupted me. 'I am *not* on my way to the park! I can't believe …' And then I realised that he was angry. He turned and glared at me. 'Esmie, I can't believe, after everything I've said, that you and Matthew would interfere like this again!'

And he went into the bathroom and slammed the door.

I was trembling. I'd thought he'd be pleased. Shocked at first, yes, but then pleased. I mean, what was so wrong with interfering in any case? Wasn't it OK to interfere if you knew that if you did, you could help someone you really loved?

'What happened?' my brother asked, looking up from his laptop as I went into his room. He'd been eating toast himself judging by all the crumbs on his bed. My eye caught our mother's photograph in the silver frame on his desk. She was smiling out at us so happily that I felt like knocking her over. I mean, what was there to smile about? Unless she was happy that everything was going wrong.

'He's really mad at us,' I said, sitting on the bed beside him. I told my brother what Dad had said. 'And he's not going to the park to see her.'

Matthew narrowed his eyes. Then he seemed to snap into action. He jumped out of bed. 'Here's what we do now, then. Listen …'

I had to admit that his determination to see our plan work out, no matter what it took, was pretty impressive. His idea was that I should go missing for a couple of hours so that Dad would have to go looking for me. 'I mean, where's the first place he's bound to look for you after what you've told him this morning?' he said, when I looked puzzled.

I thought about it for a moment, then I smiled. 'The park!'

'Exactly! Where, with any luck, Lizzie will be lying in wait for him!'

'I'll go and get dressed now,' I said, getting up. 'But I shouldn't really go down to the park, should I?'

'Of course not! We need to get Dad and Lizzie alone together. Go into town and look round the shops or something.'

I nodded, glancing again at the photograph of my mother on Matthew's desk. Her eyes were looking right at me, and it seemed like she was very, I don't know, *amused* about something. And suddenly I had a crazy thought.

Chapter Fifteen

You might not believe in heaven and all that stuff – lots of people don't – and if your mum or dad is dead you might think that the only way they can live on is in your memory. I know that's what Dad thinks. I mean, he talks to my mum sometimes because it makes him feel better to make believe that she's still there, not because he truly believes she is. At least that's what he says. Dad would probably say that the mother I talk to is sort of like an imaginary friend too, if I ever told him about her. Maybe he's right. But sometimes I reckon I can almost *feel* her watching over me and I get so that I'm almost positive that she *is* still here in some way I don't really understand. And if she is, then what if she can interfere in our lives from up in heaven?

I left the house without telling anyone and walked down the road to the bus stop. The bus didn't take long to come and it wasn't very busy so I got the seat right at the front on the top deck, which is my favourite place because you can see everything. I stayed on while the bus drove through the town and then, just before it veered off on to the ring road, I got off. It was just a short walk to the cemetery. There's a little newsagent on the way where you can buy flowers. I know because we always go at Christmas time and on my mother's birthday.

They only had some old bunches of carnations in a bucket outside the shop so I bought a Bounty bar instead. Dad told me once that my mother really liked them.

Inside the cemetery there are loads of gravestones, but I know where my mother's is. I don't know what I expected to find there but I found her grave looking the same as normal, with the jam jar still there from the last time we'd come. The jar was turned over on its side and was full of rainwater and there were some dead flowers still hanging out. I wondered if Dad came here on his own sometimes without telling us. These flowers looked like they had died too recently to be the ones we'd brought last time we all came together. I tipped up the jar so it was free of brown water and dead flowers and put it back in front of the grave sitting upright. Carefully, I balanced the Bounty bar across the top of the jar and sat back on the grass. It was a bit damp but I didn't care. I looked around quickly. There was nobody here but me.

'You don't have to worry about us forgetting you,' I said out loud, 'if that's what it is. I mean, if it's *you* who's been making everything go wrong.' I waited to see if she was going to reply. I would have freaked out if I'd heard her voice calling down to me from heaven but if I sat with my eyes shut I might find myself *thinking* her answer. Because I liked to think that was her way of communicating with me – by putting her thoughts into my head sometimes – like the thought that she still loved me even though she was dead. But my mother's voice was silent even though I screwed up my forehead and concentrated really hard.

The more I concentrated the more my mind went blank. Maybe my mother wasn't here after all. I thought about what Dad would think if he knew I was doing this. I wondered if he was worried about me now. I felt guilty thinking that he was. Maybe he'd met up with Lizzie and they were hunting for me together.

'It's not that I don't still wish you were here,' I told my mother. 'If you were, then I wouldn't want Lizzie at all. So if you can come back to us, come back now, and I'll stop looking for another mother, I promise.'

And when I said it out loud, it really hit me how much I'd been looking for a new mum for myself, rather than a new wife for Dad. I'd been trying to select her on the basis of how much *I* liked her, rather than how much Dad did. And that was the problem. Dad was angry because of the way we were sticking our noses in and telling him who was best for him as if he didn't have any right to decide that for himself. Maybe he felt a bit like *I* do when Holly tries to take over and do stuff all the time that's meant to help *me*.

I stared at my mother's name written in gold letters on the grey marble. Maybe she was up in heaven helping me to think things through. Or perhaps not. Either way, I was pretty sure she'd have wanted Dad to be happy, whether that meant him getting married again or not.

I looked at the Bounty bar sitting on top of the empty jam jar. I hadn't had any breakfast and I was pretty hungry. And suddenly it seemed really silly to leave it here for my mother when there was no way she was ever going to be able to come back to life and eat it.

I got back to find the front door wide open and Matty standing in the hall waiting for me. He must have seen me walking up the street.

'It worked!' he grinned. 'Dad's been going mental wondering where you are! I told him he'd really upset you! He's gone down the park looking for you! You'd better ring him and let him know you're safe.'

I looked at my watch. It was quarter to twelve. 'Do you think he's found Lizzie?' I asked, anxiously.

'We'll soon find out.' He watched me dial Dad's mobile number. 'So where did you go?'

I didn't answer. I was concentrating on listening to Dad's phone ringing out.

'Yes?' He sounded tense as he answered.

'Dad, it's me.'

'Esmie! Where are you? Are you at home?' He practically shouted it.

'Yes,' I said.

'Well, stay there. I'm on my way back.' And he cut me off.

'I hope he's not going to ground me,' I said, gloomily, to my brother. 'He didn't sound too happy.'

'Let's just hope he's met up with her and everything's gone all right,' Matty replied.

I spent the next ten minutes pacing up and down, wondering what was going to happen when Dad got back. But before Dad arrived home, Juliette did. She gave me a kiss on both cheeks as she walked in the door and stopped short when she saw my face. 'What has happened *now?*' But there was no time to answer her because at that moment Dad appeared at the bottom of our drive. Lizzie wasn't with him.

Matthew and I looked at him anxiously. Dad looked stern and as soon as he clapped eyes on me, he put his hand on my shoulder, turned me round and marched me into the living room where I got the biggest grilling ever about where I'd been, and lots of threats about what he'd do to me if I ever left the house without telling him again. I told him I'd only gone to look round the shops and that Holly's mum says he can't wrap us up in cotton wool for ever, but that just got him ranting on about the numbers of children who get abducted from shopping centres until Matthew said, 'Yeah, but who would want to abduct *her?*', which made Dad round on him instead.

'I'd forget the smart talk if I were you, Matthew! Didn't know where your sister was, eh?'

He went on at us both for a bit longer. Neither of us dared to ask him about Lizzie. But, just as Matty and I were giving up all hope of her even having been in the park, he suddenly told my brother he wanted him to stay in and look after me the following evening because he was going out.

'Can't Juliette do it?' Matthew protested.

'Juliette does enough babysitting. Anyway, it won't hurt you to make yourself useful!'

'Dad, where are you going?' I butted in, excitedly. 'Are you going out with anyone we *know*?'

'I *could* tell you that, Esmie,' Dad said, turning to look at me. 'But if I did, I'd be rather afraid that you might interfere and ruin everything. Without meaning to, of course.' He gave me a wry smile and suddenly I had a feeling that he wasn't quite as angry as he was making out. 'Now … I need to speak to Juliette.'

Juliette was in the kitchen, and the second Dad had left the room, Matthew and I followed him. We stood outside the door, listening.

'Juliette,' Dad said, 'I think I owe you an apology.' Matthew and I held in our breaths. Was this it? Was he about to ask her to stay? 'I'm very sorry about all those things I said before. I know you were only trying to help, even if your methods were a bit misguided. I shouldn't have spoken to you like that – it was quite uncalled for.'

'Well …' Juliette began. I could tell she had no intention of accepting his apology particularly graciously, or of apologising back, but fortunately Dad didn't seem to expect her to.

'I wonder if we could have a talk about things,' he said. 'In private.' He suddenly came to the door and stuck his head out at us as if he knew we'd been listening all along and had intended us to hear his apology but wasn't about to let us hear anything else. 'OK, you two! Upstairs! *Now!*' he barked, and we fled.

I was sure he had asked her to stay, but you can never be entirely sure about anything – as I was fast discovering – and every time I tried to talk to Juliette about it she changed the subject. Matty said that maybe Dad had asked her and she was taking some time to think about it, but I didn't see why she'd need to do that. After all, why wouldn't she want to stay now that everything was sorted out between her and Dad?

Then, the following morning, Dad woke up with pains in his tummy. Juliette reckoned he was just nervous about that evening – she was convinced that it actually *was* a date – but I wasn't so sure that was the reason. When Dad's nervous, he's just *nervous*. He never gets pains. He made a few trips to the bathroom that really stunk the place out but that didn't seem to help his tummy any because he ended up taking himself back to bed. Juliette went and got some tablets from the chemist and he took those. Then he said he was starting to feel feverish.

'You are not going to be able to go out tonight after all,' Juliette said.

Dad moaned that he *had* to. 'If I don't, she'll think I'm just chickening out. After everything else that's happened, she's never going to believe I'm really sick.' And that's when we knew that his date had to be Lizzie.

'Did you meet up with her in the park, Dad?' I pressed him. 'What happened? What did you talk about?' But he ignored me and hugged his tummy miserably.

'Then you must invite her here!' Juliette said.

'Here?' Dad grunted. 'To see me like *this*?'

'*I* will invite her. I will tell her you are sick but you need cheering up and I shall ask her to come and visit you. Have you got her number?'

But Dad refused to give it to her. 'If there's any phoning to be done, Juliette, I think I'd better do it myself,' he said, drily. 'Don't you?'

And Juliette had to admit that he had a point.

Chapter Sixteen

When the doorbell rang that evening I rushed to answer it. 'Lizzie!' I yelled out, excitedly. 'I knew you'd come! Dad met you in the park, didn't he?'

'Hello, Esmie. How's the patient?' Lizzie smiled, ignoring my question.

'Still poorly,' I said, beckoning her in. 'But he's not running to the loo as often now.'

'Good! But maybe he's not up to seeing visitors yet? Perhaps I shouldn't have come.'

'Of course he's up to seeing *you*!' I answered, eagerly, and I'd have pushed her straight up the stairs if Juliette hadn't come out into the hall and ushered her into the living room instead.

'I was just making a cup of tea,' Juliette said. 'Would you like one? I will go and tell the invalid you are here.' She winked at me as she left the room.

Now that Lizzie and I were alone together, I suddenly felt awkward. 'You'd better not give him those,' I said, as she put a bag of grapes down on the coffee table. 'Fruit isn't very good for you when you've got an upset tummy.'

Lizzie smiled. 'You're probably right, Esmie. Maybe you should have them instead.'

'OK!' I reached out and grabbed one. I love grapes. I had eaten several and was reaching out to take some more when Juliette came back.

'Wash them!' she ordered, smacking my hand. 'And put them on a plate!' She shuddered. 'I hate how the English eat grapes. Picking them off one by one. I must buy some grape scissors for this family.'

'She hates it if you cut the *nose* off the cheese as well,' I said, rolling my eyes upwards to show how daft I thought *that* was. 'You know – the pointy bit at the end.'

Lizzie laughed. 'So how are you managing, Juliette? Is your patient giving you a lot of trouble?'

Juliette pulled a face to say that she was managing, but only just. 'So irritable when he is sick! I tell him that I do not expect him to behave like a grumpy child with me, please, but he is still impossible!'

Dad arrived then. He was fully dressed, thank goodness, though I noticed he was wearing a very loose pair of trousers. He looked pretty horrible, and I just hoped we hadn't made a terrible mistake letting Lizzie see him like that. I mean, what if it put her off for ever? 'Hello, there,' he said, looking a bit nervous.

'Lizzie's brought you some grapes,' I told him. 'They're really nice but I said you'd better not eat them. Remember what Granny's always saying fruit does to her bowels.'

'I think we can do without hearing about your grand-mother's bowels, thank you, Esmie,' Dad said, wincing as he obviously got some sort of nasty spasm in *his*.

'Are you sure you wouldn't rather I left and came back another time?' Lizzie said, anxiously. 'You don't look at all well.'

'Dad's *always* really brave when he's not well,' I said, proudly. 'Holly's mum says you'd think the whole British police force was going to fall apart without him, the way he insists on going in to work even when he's sick. Holly's my best friend,' I told Lizzie. 'Her mum's single too but Dad doesn't fancy her, do you, Dad?'

'Esmie, why don't you go and see if Juliette wants any help in the kitchen?' Dad said, glaring at me.

'But Juliette's not in the –' I protested, but then I real-ised she must have slipped out of the room without me noticing.

'It's all right, really,' Lizzie said, smiling warmly at both of us. 'You stay if you want to, Esmie.'

'OK!' I said, ignoring the fact that Dad was still jerking his head at me in the direction of the kitchen. I looked at Lizzie instead. She was wearing a really nice green skirt. 'My new dress is that colour,' I told her. 'Juliette helped me choose it. Do you want to see it?'

'I'd love to!' Lizzie smiled.

'What a good idea!' Dad agreed. 'Why don't you try it on for us – and take your time! There's no rush!'

'It's OK, it won't take a minute!' I said, jumping up and running upstairs to get changed. I saw that Matty's door was closed so I stopped and knocked loudly. 'Matty! She's here!' When he didn't answer, I flung his door open.

He was listening to music. He took off his headphones and looked up. 'What?'

'Lizzie's here. And they're getting on really well!'

He grinned and gave me the thumbs-up sign. 'Good one, partner!'

'So,' Juliette's voice sounded suddenly, from halfway up the stairs. 'You are not arguing for once. That is good.' She came up behind me and put her hand on my shoulder. 'It looks as though our Lonely Hearts Plan has worked out after all, no?'

I nodded. 'Juliette, you *are* going to stay, now, aren't you?' I asked her, earnestly. 'I mean, that's what Dad wanted to talk to you about the other day, wasn't it?'

'Yes,' she said. 'Your father has asked me to stay.'

'Great!' I laughed. 'Now everything's perfect!'

'I have decided to stay,' Juliette continued, quickly, 'on one condition.'

I looked at her. 'What?'

'The condition is that you remember, Esmie, that I will not be staying for ever. I will only be here until the end of the year, then it will be time for me to go.'

'Of course, but that's ages away,' I said, dismissively. Juliette was staying on *now*, and that was all that mattered to me at the moment.

But Juliette seemed to be really worried about something. 'Esmie, I do not want you to think of me as always being here with you,' she went on, slowly. 'It worries me that you … What I mean is that I cannot …' She paused, frowning. 'I cannot be your mother,' she said, finally. 'Nobody can. Different people can fill that gap a little bit but nobody can be the perfect mother you have in your dreams.'

'I know,' I said. 'Except that Lizzie seems really nice and if Dad really likes her and they fall in love and get married … I mean, I know they might not but –'

'Even if you eventually end up with the best step-mother in the world, she will not be perfect,' Juliette interrupted me. 'And I do not want you to expect her to be.' She sighed. 'Esmie, even if you had a real mother, she would not be the one you dream of inside your head. The mothers we make up in our heads are always perfect. Even people with real mothers have imaginary ones too, and the imaginary ones make it really difficult for the real ones to do anything right!'

'What do you mean?' I frowned. I'd never thought before that other people might have make-believe mothers too.

'Think about it,' Juliette replied, firmly.

So I promised that I would think about it. But not now. *Now*, all I wanted was to put on my new dress and dance about the house in it.

Suddenly Matthew spoke. 'Don't worry about us, Juliette. We'll be OK.'

Juliette gave him a tender look. 'You are a sweet boy, Matthew.'

My brother looked embarrassed and quickly put his headphones back on.

'What about me?' I asked, anxiously. 'Am *I* sweet too?'

'I thought you did not like to be called "sweet"!' Juliette laughed. 'I thought Holly's mother said –'

'Holly's mother doesn't know everything!' I interrupted, huffily, as I flounced off to my own room to get changed.

Chapter Seventeen

There's not a whole lot more to tell you really, except that Dad and Lizzie are still getting on really well and it's been over three months now. Lizzie comes round to our place a lot and sometimes she does stuff just with me, like she takes me shopping or we go and see some girlie film together. Juliette was right, though – she's not perfect. She gets all het up when she's driving and you can't get her to pay you any attention at all if she's trying to pass a traffic light before it turns back to red, and she parks in places where she shouldn't which gets *Dad* all het up. She isn't a very good cook, either. So far as I can tell she can only make two things – lasagne and chilli con carne – and otherwise she just buys stuff out of Marks and Spencer. But at least she seems to make Dad happy.

Matthew and Jake are friends again, and Jake has completely stopped hanging out with those other boys.

Matty says he reckons Jake gave himself a fright when he stole those CDs. I said that I wasn't going to speak to Jake again unless he took the CDs back to the shop and owned up, but Matthew said that Jake couldn't be expected to be *that* brave and that maybe I should give him a break just so long as he promised never to steal anything again. Anyway, now the two of them have started going to Burger King after school instead of McDonald's, ever since a girl in their class told Matty that she always goes there after school with her friends. I reckon Matthew fancies her, and when I asked him, he told me to shut up and went bright red, which Holly says definitely confirms it.

Matthew and Dad are planning to paint Matthew's bedroom together. It was Juliette who suggested that and Lizzie thinks it's a good idea too. Matty wants to paint the walls black so he's arguing with Dad about *that* now. Matthew says that *he* doesn't find black a depressing colour and that it's *his* room so he ought to be able to paint it whatever colour he likes.

'I suppose Jake is painting *his* room black as well, is he?' Dad said, drily, as they had yet another discussion about it over breakfast the other day.

'I *can* do stuff without Jake having to do it first, Dad!' my brother snapped, looking cross.

'You could've fooled me,' I put in, loudly. (I say that to my brother a lot now. Holly started me on it and I've discovered that it really annoys Matty, especially if I throw in a dismissive little shoulder shrug to go with it.)

Matty whirled round to glare at me. 'Esmie, you are so ... so ...' He seemed to be struggling to find a word that was sufficiently horrible to describe me, so I made a big thing of sitting waiting, cupping my face in my hands and resting my elbows on the table while I smiled up at him sweetly.

Dad laughed. 'I do believe we have another teenager on the way!' he said, pulling a face of mock horror at the thought. 'Now, Matthew, about this decorating ... Your bedroom *does* belong to you – the space *between* the walls. The walls however are all mine – and they're staying a normal colour. Got it?'

I rolled my eyes. Juliette is right. Their arguing *is* boring.

I found Juliette sitting in the living room. The free paper was open in front of her and some of the adverts on the lonely-hearts page were circled.

'I am fed up with these *pathetic* Englishmen who are too *scared* to ask me out,' she said. 'I am thinking of putting in an advert myself. What do you think?'

'*Juliette seeks Romeo …*' I giggled.

She frowned. 'I shall not be putting *that,*' she said, firmly. 'I shall be putting something far more sophisticated. I just cannot think *what.*'

'How about this?' I said, grabbing some paper and composing what I reckoned was the perfect ad for Juliette.

'You really think that describes *me?*' Juliette gasped, when she had read it.

'Oh, yes!' I laughed. 'Definitely! And you'll get so many replies, you're bound to fall in love with one of them and then you won't want to go back to France after all!'

'Esmie, I have something for you,' Juliette suddenly said, jumping up. It turned out she'd bought me the DVD of *Mary Poppins.* 'I thought we could watch it this afternoon, just the two of us.' One of Dad's friends had got hold of some tickets for a football match that afternoon so Dad and Matthew were going together.

We waited until they'd left and then Juliette and I settled down to watch *Mary Poppins* together. I really enjoyed it, especially when they ride the horses on the merry-go-round and all the horses take off and end up on the racecourse and Mary Poppins ends up winning the race. And I loved the bit where everyone goes floating up to the ceiling and the part at the end when the children's dad starts noticing them at last. But when it got to the bit where Mary Poppins had to go home, I started to feel really sad. I mean, I knew that it was time for her to go because she'd fixed everything by then, but the children were still going to miss her really badly.

'Do you think she'll ever come back and see them?' I asked Juliette, in a small voice, as the film finished.

'Of course she will,' Juliette replied, firmly. 'Those children will always be special to her! She will never forget them!'

I looked at her. '*They* won't ever forget *her* either,' I said, solemnly.

'*Forget* Mary Poppins?!' Juliette gasped in horror. 'I should hope not!'

And we both started to laugh.

ALL ABOUT GWYNETH!

If you'd like to find out more about Gwyneth Rees,
check out her author page on
Facebook.com/GwynethReesAuthor
or email her on **gwyneth.rees@bloomsbury.com**.

Please make sure you that you have permission from a parent or guardian.

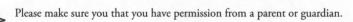

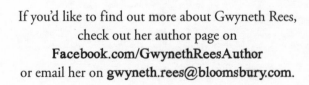

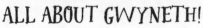